# FINDING ROMANCE

## ROMANCES IN THE BUILDING SERIES
### BOOK 2

## S.E. ROSE

# COPYRIGHT



Editing by Judy's Proofreading
Couple Illustration © Celia Moscote
Cover Design by S.E. Rose

# DEDICATION

To anyone who ever felt a little lost in life. Keep going. You never know when you might find yourself on the perfect path for you.

And to a certain individual who asked if I had used your real life in any stories. Honestly, your real life deserves its own story, but I did get some inspiration for Kasen from you.

# CHAPTER ONE

Kasen

"Where the hell have you been?" Hutch asks as I'm surrounded by my neighbors. I feel like I've been gone for eons. In reality, it's been less than twelve weeks. A very long twelve weeks.

Al, the owner of our apartment building, hands me my favorite whiskey and I raise it toward him in a cheers motion.

"Welcome home, Kase," he says with his patented grandfatherly smile.

"My grandmother was ill, and just as I was ready to leave on my next assignment, her friend called to say she had fallen. So, I went to stay with her until she was all better," I explained. I don't explain how my boss was cool about it and how I had to hand two projects off to fellow colleagues. I hated doing it and I feel like shit because I wasn't there, being a team player.

"And you couldn't like, I don't know, text us back?" Hutch says with a raised eyebrow.

I grimace because I feel like a jerk. Out of all my neighbors, I'm closest to Hutch and I should have texted him. I left in such a hurry, I didn't grab my UK SIM card. I barely had time to grab my UK passport. And while I could have gone in search of another SIM card a few weeks ago, I decided against it. I had already spent over two months on the remote island where Gran lives without good cell service and Wi-Fi. By the end of it, I felt like I had stepped back in time two hundred years. And I'll be honest, I think I needed it. I needed to slow down, but now I'm back and ready to immerse myself in work and life again.

"Sorry, mate. The cell service and Wi-Fi were awful, and I did finally get your texts a few weeks ago, but I knew I would be back and figured I'd just tell you everything in person," I explain, feeling like a total asshole. If I was being honest, I'd tell him how having no contact with the outside world for weeks was therapeutic. For the first time in a long time, the world shrunk down to the person I've cared about the most. I hadn't spent that long with a family member since I was a kid, and it felt good. But I knew it would be a short-lived experience and I have to get my head back in the game.

"Damn, where does she live, an outpost in Siberia?" he asks. A few of my neighbors chuckle.

"Hutch, do you ever listen to anything? She lives in Scotland," Brayden says. There are five of us younger guys in the building. Brayden, Grayson, Hutch, Drew, and me. And we have become thick as thieves, in addition to Cam and Carly, and Carly's daughter, Ava, who has taken up residence on my lap. I've missed this kid. She's the coolest.

In addition to the young people, we have Jessa and Troy, our building's parental figures who take care of all things electric and plumbing-related. Margie and Cornelia are like our grandmothers or crazy great-aunts and Al, well, he's the reason we are all here. He's like the godfather of one-eleven Hearts Lane.

Hutch slaps his forehead. "Damn, sorry, I forgot. So, you took your UK passport. This all makes so much more sense. God, I'm an idiot. I can't believe I didn't remember that."

I see our new tenant give him a look. I also see Gray squeezing her shoulder. Clearly, I have lots to catch up on.

She rolls her eyes and extends her hand. "I'm Roxy, by the way."

"Nice to meet you. I take it you are the owner of the bookshop downstairs?" I say as I put two and two together. I'd seen the bookstore as I came back into the building and I know that when I left and told Al I'd be gone a few weeks, he reminded me that the new tenant was moving in while I was away. I guess I should have told Al more about what I was doing because everyone seems a little freaked out by my long absence. Good to know my friends care that much.

She nods and gives me a warm smile and I immediately like her. "Guilty. Hope you like romance novels."

I press my lips together to keep my answer from escaping my mouth because I most definitely am not a fan of them.

She laughs. "I'm teasing. I already guessed it wasn't your genre, but if you change your mind, the boys here are all reading a billionaire romance that Cam recommended."

I nearly spit out my whiskey. "I'm sorry, what?" I look around at my friends.

"For research purposes," Gray clarifies.

"Research?" I ask, my brows furrowing. What in the hell has happened here since I left? Never in my wildest dreams would I have envisioned my friends reading romance novels for research.

Hutch claps me on the back. "Bro, you have missed a shit ton. Have a seat and fill us in on your life and then we'll catch you up to speed."

I hand Ava a colored pencil that's rolled across the bar top. "There's not much to catch you all up on. Gran was sick and fell and hurt her foot. I stepped in to help. And that's basically all I've been doing. I had some colleagues step in and help with my projects since I could not do anything. Now, you tell me what has been going on here." I feel bad not telling them more, but it really was as simple as what I said. Did I have a near panic attack about Gran? Yes. Did I worry about leaving her? Yes. Did she have to practically boot me off the island? Yes. I'm still worried about her. I hate that she's out there alone. I know she has friends and neighbors, but it's not the same as when I'm there.

Drew clears his throat, and I turn to look at him. "The summary version is that Roxy finally moved in downstairs. She opened the romance bookstore down there. Gray scored a major motion picture and there was a little fib told to the producer who thought he had a girlfriend. Al talked Roxy into going on a blind date to help a friend out, which turned out to be Gray and it also turned out to be at the film's post-production party. So, the two fake dated and then that turned into a real dating situation and, well, the rest is history. Oh, and Cam might try to buy the bakery soon. And Hutch is still trying to figure out who leaves the flowers on the bench at the park every day. And I think that sums up everything."

"Wow. Well, I suppose I have been gone for three months. That's a lot. Cheers to the new happy couple," I say as I hold my glass up to Roxy and Gray. A twinge of jealousy coats me but I squash it down with a smile.

Everyone yells "cheers." And just like that, I'm back where I belong.

# CHAPTER TWO

Piper

"When's the surgery?" I ask as I hang up a dress in my closet.

"Tuesday," my great-aunt replies. I pause and try to remember what day it is. I've been sleeping in my old bedroom at my mother's house since I graduated from art school six months ago. My mom is an ultra-marathoner. She's always running in a race or organizing one. This week, she's in the Florida Keys which is probably why my great-aunt is calling me to come help her after her surgery. Her sister, my grandmother, wouldn't be much help. She walks with a cane now and doesn't climb stairs any longer.

I must pause for too long because she adds, "You can stay as long as you want. I should be recovered in a month."

"Uh, sure. I can be there. How's Margie?" I ask, inquiring about her roommate. The two of them are thick as thieves. Margie might as well be another great-aunt to me at this point. I think the two of them have lived there together for almost ten years since both of their husbands passed away.

"Oh, she's good. Her gout is acting up again, but otherwise, she's busy knitting a new sweater. I bet she'd make you one," Aunt Cornelia says.

"Shall I pick us up some of that green tea you liked?" I say as I pull my suitcase from the closet and start tossing things into it. My great-aunt lives about an hour and a half away, so I could come and go, but it would be easier to just stay there for a few weeks, especially if she needs help at night. If she's calling me, then she must really need the help. My great-aunt is a stubborn woman and I'm one hundred percent sure she turned down professional help because that is something she would totally do. But since I'm not working, I guess it's the least I can do to help a woman who means so much to me.

"That would be lovely, dear. Feel free to come over whenever. I have to be at the hospital at six in the morning for the surgery. They wrapped up my ankle real well last night, but I can't put any pressure on it," Aunt Cornelia explains.

For fuck's sake, I need to be there today. There's no way Margie can help her get to the bathroom. I'd never forgive myself if both of them ended up injured. My aunt apparently tripped over a basket of her crocheting yarn and somehow managed to break her ankle. They splinted it and sent her home. Fortunately, her friend from bingo is an orthopedic surgeon and already got her scheduled for surgery.

"I'm packing up now and will be there in about two hours, OK?" I reply as I grab my toiletries and throw them in a bag. I have no idea what to bring. I'm currently an unemployed artist with a degree and zero job prospects. It'd probably be a good thing to get out of Mom's house for a few weeks. I'm sure she misses her solitary life. My mom is great, but she's also not super social. Maybe that's why she loves running by herself for insanely long distances as if she can run from having to speak to people.

I smile as I zip my suitcase. It will be nice to spend time

with Margie and Aunt Cornelia. They are hilarious and give the best advice. Hell, maybe they can help me find a job.

"You are the best. Poor Margie is having a tough time helping me move around. We'll see you soon," she says.

"Bye," I reply as I hang up and finish packing.

It doesn't take me long to get my things together, mostly because I don't have many things. I get in my car, a high school graduation gift from my father who lives in another state and only talks to me on holidays and birthdays. He mostly spends his free time with his girlfriend, traveling the world. Last week, I got a postcard from Bali. I guess I should be happy that I get the two-line cards when he visits destinations that he'd never take me to. Heck, I'd be happy if he showed up and took me to a ballgame like he used to when I was a kid. But those outings died with the divorce.

Divorced parents as a solo kid is a lonely place to be. Especially when your parents went out and found lives without you. In high school, I liked being independent and enjoyed the alone time, but now, I could use some parental advice.

I press the call button on my steering wheel as I drive out of the neighborhood and onto the nearby interstate.

"What's wrong?" Mom answers.

"Nothing, well, sort of nothing. Aunt Cornelia fell and broke her ankle," I explain.

I hear Mom sigh. "Is she alright?"

"Yeah, she's fine. I'm going to stay with her and Margie to help out for a few weeks," I state as I merge into traffic, heading towards the city and leaving the leafy suburbs behind. It's sort of exciting. I love going to the city.

"Well, that's nice of you, sweetheart. Give her my best. I'll be back next Saturday and then the following Thursday I leave for that conference in Las Vegas," she says.

"Good luck with the race tomorrow," I say. Mom has a

whole team of runner friends and they support each other in these crazy races. I've gone several times, but I always found I was more in the way than assisting.

"Thank you. I'll have Denise text you throughout it and then I'll call when I'm rested afterward," she says.

"OK, love ya," I say.

"Love you too," she replies, and I know she means it, but also I feel like she says it out of obligation. We have a strange relationship, but at least she's there for me when I really need her and not just for graduations and award ceremonies like my father is.

———

I look up at the six-story brick building and then back down, noticing a bookstore that has opened in the small commercial space on the ground floor. I'll have to check that out.

Aunt Cornelia and Margie live on the fourth floor. There's no way she's getting up and down if the elevator breaks.

I haven't hung out here in a long time. I used to come visit when I was a teenager but that was years ago. I know Al who owns the building still lives on the top floor and I'm pretty sure Troy and Jessa still live here and help out with the building maintenance and administration stuff, but I don't really know any of the other tenants. I think there was a doctor here when I stayed for a weekend in high school, but I was too busy on my phone to pay much attention at the time. And I've only popped by twice while in college. Cornelia usually comes to visit my grandmother and that's where I've seen her lately.

I shut my car door and grab my backpack and suitcase. As I go to press the buzzer, a man comes up behind me.

"You visiting someone?" he asks as he uses a key to get inside the small lobby.

"Oh, yep, my aunt Cornelia," I say.

He holds out a hand as we wait in front of the lobby. "I'm Brayden. I think I remember you from a long time ago. You were in high school."

"You're the doctor," I remember with a smile as we get into the small space of the elevator and I hope it makes it up to the fourth floor. I press the button and silently pray to the elevator gods.

"I am," he replies with a grin.

"I'm Piper," I say.

"I heard Cornelia fell. I wasn't working when she came into the ER. I'll stop in with you and see how she is. If she needs anything, I'm just a floor below her," he says.

"Thanks, that's really nice of you," I say as the doors open and we step out into the small hallway.

I knock on the door to number seven and Margie opens it.

"I'm so glad you're here. Your aunt needs to use the bathroom and I can't lift her," she says as she ushers us both inside.

"We got it," Brayden says as we walk into the back hallway and find my aunt lying on the sofa with her casted leg on an ottoman.

"Hey, we're here," I announce as I walk over to her.

"Let's get you to the bathroom," Brayden says as we each take an arm and help her up. Brayden gets one of those walkers with a seat from the corner of the room and we set her on it and wheel her down the hall to the bathroom. I'm not exactly a big person, but my aunt is teeny tiny. And right now as she's assuring Brayden we are good, I'm glad she's so small. I can easily help lift her to the toilet.

Once she's settled, I step outside to give her privacy.

"I'll help you get her settled. Are you sure you got this? I know a good nurse service if you need help," Brayden offers.

"I appreciate it. I think she turned one down already," I whisper. "But I used to volunteer at a nursing home, so this is a piece of cake. Plus, Aunt Cornelia is a lightweight." I flex my bicep and Brayden chuckles.

"OK, just make sure to let me know if you change your mind," he urges.

I nod and a moment later Aunt Cornelia calls me back into the bathroom. I help sponge bathe her with some wipes and then we go get her settled in her room. Brayden gives me his phone number and leaves after making sure we all know we should call if we need anything.

Aunt Cornelia suddenly yells out for me and I run back into her room. "My necklace is gone. Can you go check the hallway outside? Maybe it fell off when the ambulance came."

I want to groan and tell her it's a lost cause, but I know it's the necklace from her late husband that she always wears. I hope she didn't lose it at the hospital.

I look around the apartment and then step into the hallway. I turn around and stare at their door, looking down at the ground. I bend over and start to scoot back when I hear something and then feel a wall of human bump my ass.

"Whoa!" a deep voice says from behind and I start to sway forward. Giant hands grip my hips and I realize we must look...well, thank God no one else is here.

I get my bearings and stand, turning slowly. My eyes find a wide chest as they continue looking up, and up until they meet a bearded chin and then dark eyes. Holy shit, is this their neighbor? He's enormous. And he looks...grumpy. Fabulous, just what I need. A hot-as-hell, grumpy neighbor.

# CHAPTER THREE

Kasen

"You OK?" I mutter as I step back and take in this pixie of a woman. She's probably of average height, but the only person I know taller than me is Hutch. I tend to think everyone is small, but she's truly a wisp of a human. I could bench-press her. Her dark hair is pulled up into some sort of bun on her head. Strands are sticking in every direction. She's wearing some kind of dress with leggings. Her face is, well...she's gorgeous. Giant eyes look up at me and I study them. One is most definitely green and the other blue. There's a name for that but it fails me at the moment.

She runs her hands over her dress. "Yeah, I'm fine. Sorry, I was looking for my aunt's necklace." She motions to the ground and my eyes follow her long slender finger.

My brows furrow as I try to figure out what she means. Is she related to Margie or Cornelia?

"Who's your aunt?"

"Cornelia. Well, she's my great-aunt...I mean my grandmother's sister. Anyhow, she hurt her ankle and I'm here to help for a bit. I guess in all the excitement earlier she lost her necklace. It was from her husband. It means so much to her. I thought I might find it out here but so far no luck," she explains as she clasps her hands together and rocks on her heels. I look down and find her wearing Converse sneakers. They have little cats drawn all over them. The drawings are pretty good.

"I didn't know she had a niece," I state as I look past her to the door. "Cornelia is injured?"

I just got home a bit ago. I had a client with a server issue and I ended up having to go to the office to fix it, which of course took the whole damn night.

"Yeah, she broke her ankle and has to get surgery," she explains. "I'm Piper by the way."

She holds out her hand and I shake it. Piper. The name suits her. She looks like a little sand piper, tiny and curious.

"Kasen," I reply.

But then, her previous words hit me and I frown. "Does she need anything?" I ask. I feel like a shit neighbor. I'm hardly ever around. Margie and Cornelia have been great neighbors. They are always looking out for me. If they could reach the top of my aquarium, I'm sure they'd take care of my fish when I'm gone.

"Nah. I just got her sorted. But thanks," she says. "I should probably get back to looking."

I glance around. "I'll look out for it on my way down-stairs," I offer because not only do I feel bad, I'm also completely mesmerized by the beauty in front of me and my protective vibes have just kicked into high gear.

She nods. "Thanks." She gives me a little wave as I leave.

I make it down to Grayson's door and knock. He opens it and I step inside and immediately am greeted by a cat.

"What in the hell is that?" I ask as a black kitten rubs up against my leg.

"It's the Loch Ness Monster." He gives me a pointed look. "What do you think it is?"

"I mean, you got a cat?" Why has so much changed since I left? I feel like I've come back to a different world and it's sort of freaking me out.

"I found her. And yes, I have a cat. The computer is over here," he says and points to his laptop.

I sit down and start to go through his computer.

"I owe you a beer," he says.

"Yeah, yeah,' I mutter as I type away, looking for the issue which takes all of twenty seconds. One minute later, he's sorted.

"You coming to happy hour this week?" Gray asks as I get up and head toward his door.

"Probably," I reply. Honestly, I'm not sure I will. My head is all over the place. I need to take a few days and figure out some shit in my life.

"Cool. Maybe we can hit the gym tomorrow," Gray adds as I open the door.

"I'll be there at zero dark thirty," I reply, fighting a smirk. Gray hates getting up early. He's a night owl.

"Have fun, then. I'm not getting up until the sun does," he says as I shut the door. I had been in a shit mood, but between Cornelia's niece and Gray, I'm not feeling quite as heavy as I make my way back to my apartment and settle into my work.

---

I look out at the street for the tenth time in as many minutes. I need a coffee and the shit I make isn't cutting it. The light finally comes on at the café and I see Cam opening up things.

"About bloody time," I growl to myself as I stretch. I've already been to the gym, showered, drank my protein shake, and replied to five emails. My grandmother would be rolling her eyes at my coffee obsession. As much as I love a good cup of tea, I could never give up my coffee.

I pull on a shirt and head downstairs. The morning light is just starting to brighten the sky. I have a feeling it'll be a pretty sunrise. Maybe I'll go watch it from the rooftop. I could use a moment to clear my head before I get started with my next project. I step into the café and turn back to see Al coming out of the apartment building and looking around. He shrugs and puts his hat on as he walks toward the park trail.

I notice someone sitting on the bench. Keeping one eye on them, I glance over to see Cam watching me as I press my hands against the counter.

"Usual?" she asks.

I nod with a grunt.

"You meet Cornelia's niece yet?" she asks, motioning toward the bench.

I frown and look at her. "Have you?"

She nods. "I found her looking for Cornelia's necklace on the sidewalk this morning. Said she couldn't sleep and was going to paint. I told her to grab a drink first."

"What'd she get?" I ask because she must have gotten it quickly since it only takes a minute for me to leave my apartment and come over here.

"Black, cream, three pumps of caramel," she says as she hands me my coffee. She grins. "Black, cream, three pumps of simple syrup."

Now, to be fair, I had only ever had black coffee with two sugars, but Cam made me up my game one day and it's been my order ever since. Simple and just a little sweet.

I toss some cash down on the counter. "See you later,

Cam," I say as I leave. My legs start carrying me toward the park bench for reasons I can't understand.

The person is still sitting there, and just as Cam said, it's Cornelia's niece. She turns as I approach. I notice then that the flowers are there.

"Hey," she says, giving me a small smile.

I grunt a "hello" and she moves the flowers out of the way.

"Someone left these here. Although, I swear I remember seeing flowers here before. Weird, right?" she says as she sets the flowers to the side of the bench and pats the open area next to her.

I look over to see an easel and a painting. She's good. She's painting some flowers that are growing alongside the stream.

I'm not sure why, but I sit down.

"It needs more color, doesn't it?" she says as she leans in to study her work.

"I think it's fine," I mutter before taking a sip. I practically moan. I missed this coffee. And I don't miss things.

"You're not a talker, huh?" she asks, and then quickly adds, "Not that you have to be. I like to be quiet sometimes too."

I look over at her and she's watching me carefully.

"I highly doubt that," I say as I search her eyes. The pink emerging with the sun on the horizon reflects in the blacks of her eyes. She's stunning.

She grins. "Haha. Very funny. I'll have you know, I've been sitting here being very quiet for an hour now." She pauses and points up and I look into the sky. There are big puffy clouds that are also tinged with pink.

"Michaelangelo's time of day," she says as if that explains something.

"I don't understand," I say as I look back down at her.

She sighs and leans back on the bench.

"Have you ever seen his paintings? The clouds are like

this, dark on one side, light on another," she explains as she points above us. I look up again and it's like I'm seeing clouds for the first time. She's right. They do look like that.

"Have you seen his paintings?" I ask as I sip my coffee again.

"Yep. I studied in Rome for a semester," she states as she leans forward and starts working on her painting again.

I watch her in silence for a few minutes. She's good, very good.

"Did you find Cornelia's necklace?" I ask, breaking the calm between us.

Her shoulders slump and her hand stills. "No. Not yet. But I haven't given up yet. I've even told a few people to be on the lookout," she says before going back to painting.

I don't know if it's her defeated posture or her frown, but suddenly I feel like I'd do anything to cheer her up. "I'll help you look for it," I say before my brain can function.

"You will!" she exclaims as she stops again and turns to me. Her brush streaks across my cheek and her mouth falls open in a perfect "O" as she gasps. "Oh God! I'm so sorry. Here, let me..." She trails off as she grabs a towel and tries to clean my cheek. I reach up and grab her hand with one of mine. Damn, her fingers are so small and delicate.

"It's OK," I state. And the smile on her lips makes me want to do more to make her happy.

"And yes, I will. Next time you want to go look for it, knock," I add as I get up and walk back to the apartment building before I do something even dumber than I just did. What the hell was I thinking? Help her look for a necklace? Since when do I do things like that? Oh yeah, never, until some artsy, happy-go-lucky beauty decides to visit her aunt. I run a hand over my face. Why do I feel like I just made a big mistake?

# CHAPTER FOUR

Piper

"Don't worry about the necklace right now. It's wine night. Grab some glasses and come sit out here," Aunt Cornelia says.

This woman literally had surgery yesterday and she's already bossing me around. Hopefully, that's a good sign.

"Aunt Cornelia, you can't drink. You're on painkillers," I chastise, my hands going to my hips as I walk into the living room. I managed to get her set up on a chair with her leg on the ottoman. She glares at me, and I want to smirk but I'm tired. She may weigh nothing, but damn, it's hard helping her move around. The friend that brought over their walker that has a little seat on it and wheels also brought over a special chair for the toilet which has been useful. She can't shower for a few days, so I went and got some more wet wipes for her. At some point last night, she offered to call a nursing service if it was too much. But I can be as stubborn as her, so I told her firmly no.

"I know that. But that doesn't mean everyone else can't have some," she says with a long sigh.

I pat her shoulder. "Sorry. Maybe you'll be off pain meds by next week."

"I hope so," she grumbles as Margie comes in and sets some tea down on the small stand next to her. "What's that?" she asks as she points to the mug.

"Vanilla red tea. You'll like it. I added simple syrup," Margie says with a big smile.

My aunt rolls her eyes, and I turn around to hide my grin.

There's a knock on the door and I leave the two older women to discuss the plusses and minuses of red tea. I open it and am surprised to see Kasen standing there.

"Oh, hey," I manage as I look up at him. "Do you need something?"

"No, but I think you need something." He turns and points to the open door behind him. I peer around him and see a chair.

Frowning, I look back at him. "Uh, I..." I trail off because I have no idea what to say.

"I have one of those chairs that lifts you to help you stand. It also lies flat, well, nearly flat. I thought Cornelia might like to borrow it," he explains.

"You rang?" a voice calls out as a giant, blond man comes up the stairs.

"Hutch, you want to help carry this," Kasen asks the man. I feel like I've met him before, maybe when I visited a few years ago.

"Oh, hey, you're Piper, right?" Hutch asks as he extends a hand, well, it's more a giant mitt. Then it dawns on me. He's the football player and I did meet him a few years ago but he was sitting down and we only spoke for a few minutes since I had to leave to go attend a friend's photo exhibit downtown.

"Yep. I think we met a while back, yes?" I ask him,

confirming that I'm not making up something in my head, which seems entirely possible because I haven't exactly slept great since being here. I thought I had to pee a lot but Aunt Cornelia needs to get up at least twice in the night.

He smiles and it puts me at ease. Something is calming about Hutch, like he's a giant but he wouldn't hurt a fly. I make a mental note to think of Hutch as a gentle giant. Especially when he picks up what has to be a several-hundred-pound chair with ease and Kasen guides it through the door of my aunt's apartment. Hutch sets it next to the one Aunt Cornelia is sitting in and then sits down in it.

Patting the armrests, he looks around. "I think you'll like the view better in this chair," he states. Then he stands and leans over Aunt Cornelia. "May I?" he asks as he looks from her to the chair.

"Hutch, you better be gentle. I'm old," she protests.

"Ma'am, I'm always gentle," he says with a wink as he scoops her up and then, true to his word, cautiously sets her down in the fancy chair.

He presses a button on the remote and the leg rest moves up, supporting the cast on her leg. He leans in and shows her how it works, including a heat option and a massage option.

"This is heaven," Aunt Cornelia declares as she vibrates with the chair.

We all laugh.

"OK, well, feel free to keep that until you are all recovered," Kasen says as he walks back over to the door and Hutch joins him.

"Thank you, sweat pea," Aunt Cornelia says. "But if you think for one minute I'm giving you back this chair, you have another thing coming."

He chuckles and walks out with Hutch in tow.

"Oh, keep a lookout for my necklace, boys!" she calls out after them.

"We will," Kasen replies as he shuts the door.

I'm about to bring in a charcuterie board that Margie's prepared when there's a knock at the door.

"The ladies are here," my aunt says, and for the first time in days, I see a real smile grace her lips.

I open the door to find four women standing there. Two are holding bottles of wine, one has a fruit salad, and another has a plate of cookies.

"Hello," I say, recognizing some of them from around the building, but not all of them. I step back as they file inside.

"Girls, this is my niece, Piper," Aunt Cornelia says as Margie brings in the cheese platter and sets it at arm's length of her.

Margie points out each woman. "This is Carly. She lives across from Brayden and has an adorable little girl, Ava. This is Cam. She works at the café across the street and makes the best baked goods. But, you girls met already, yes?" We both nod. "This is Roxy. Roxy owns the bookstore downstairs. And this is Jocelyn. She works at the bookstore. We are down one tonight. Jessa is meeting an old friend for dinner. But you know her."

I nod. Jessa and Troy have lived here longer than my aunt and Margie. Cam wanders into the kitchen and comes back out with wineglasses for everyone. And before I know it, all the women are settled on seats and chatting about all the juicy neighborhood gossip. I can see why my aunt loves this place.

"So, Gray is taking me away next weekend, but I have no idea where. Did he tell any of you?" Roxy asks.

I purse my lips. "Gray, the composer who lives downstairs?" I ask, confirming because it's been a hot minute since I've seen him.

She nods. "That'd be the one."

"Nope. You know he wouldn't trust us with that information, right?" Carly says with a giggle.

"Did anyone ever get the scoop on where Kasen's been?" Jocelyn asks. My ears perk up at the name of the mysterious, grumpy man across the hall.

"Sort of, but just what he told everyone at happy hour," Roxy says.

"I just feel like, there has to be more to that story," Jocelyn laments with a sigh before taking a long sip of a merlot.

Cam shrugs. "Who knows? That man could be James Bond for all we know."

"True," Carly says as she reaches for the chardonnay.

"Who's watching Ava tonight?" Margie asks.

"Bray for the first part and Kasen for the second part," she says.

"Huh?" I ask, confused.

"Oh, Bray has to work tonight, but he promised Ava that they would finish this puzzle they've been working on. Kasen volunteered to get her to bed." Carly snorts a little as she laughs and the others join in, including me, because the thought of Kasen tucking in a small child is pretty funny.

"What, no Hutch?" Cam asks while grabbing a piece of cheese. I reach for some myself because I've flat-out forgotten to eat tonight. I definitely chose correctly when I went to art school and not nursing school. Taking care of someone is hard work.

"Nah, he promised his brother that they'd play some video game tonight," Carly explains.

"Everyone here is, like, really close, huh?" I ask because I'm truly curious. I remember my aunt taking me up to some happy hour thing on the rooftop once as a teenager. And they are always talking about their neighbors, but I never realized just how tight-knit the building is.

"Yep," Roxy says with a grin.

Cam throws a cracker at her and rolls her eyes. Roxy laughs. "Some of us are closer than others," Cam states dryly.

"Hey, don't be a jealous beotch!" Roxy retorts.

Cam groans. "Anyhow, do you have a significant other?" Everyone looks at me.

"Oh, uh, no," I stumble over the words too quickly. I feel my cheeks heat a little. Every woman my age seems way more experienced with men than me. While most girls were dating in high school, I was flip-flopping between my parents' homes and then spending time with my grandmother, my aunt, or an art camp. And now, I'm a twenty-three-year-old virgin. Talk about feeling inadequate. I wouldn't know the first thing about doing anything but kissing a boy and that's only happened a few times. I can literally count the number of dates I've been on with my two hands. I had one college roommate who tried to get me out on dates with guys she knew, but none of them worked out. The guys were terrible kissers and just wanted in my pants immediately, or they were super jerks and we never even got to the kissing part of the date. By junior year, I just put dating on the back burner, figuring it would happen after college, but here I am nearly six months out of college, and I still haven't dated anyone.

"Well, you're young. No rush, right?" Cam offers.

I nod a little and take a sip of wine so I can keep from talking. Carly's phone pings, and she smiles and walks to the front window.

"May I?" she asks my aunt and Margie. They nod and everyone grins. I'm confused until she opens the window, pokes her head out, and looks up.

"Goodnight, Mommy!" Ava yells. I smile.

"Yeah, goodnight, Mommy," Kasen mimics.

We all burst into laughter. "Goodnight, everyone else," Ava yells again.

"Make good choices," Kasen adds.

Shaking her head, Carly closes the window. She turns to us and Roxy says, "I think we need to find that man a girlfriend."

"Agree," everyone else says in unison before Margie brings up a book she wants to read and Roxy and Jocelyn start talking about the author. I sit back and listen, wishing I had friends like this who would find me a boyfriend. I guess I'll just add it to the list of things I need to find that include a place of my own to live and a job. Those two seem way more likely than the boyfriend thing.

# CHAPTER FIVE

Kasen

"So, you home for a while?" Hutch asks as he spots me. Hutch and I have a routine when I'm home. Three times a week, we get up at zero dark thirty and walk the two blocks to the local gym. Sometimes Bray, Drew, or Gray joins us, but more often than not, it's just us.

I put the bar back in its holder and look up at my friend. Hutch is a good man. While most see him as silly and kind, I know the serious side of him, the part of him he doesn't often share with others.

"For now," I reply as I get up and switch places with him.

"Good. It's not the same around here without you," he huffs as he grabs the bar and begins his set.

I glare at him, and he grins up at me. I can understand how he's a magnet with the women. But it's strange he's not had a single serious relationship since living here.

I know he's had a tough time since the accident. And I'm sure he'd be a good person to confide in, but I'm not sure I'm ready to air all my dirty laundry, not even to a man I consider to be one of my closest friends. Sometimes, I feel like a stranger in my own life. But part of me likes that. I'm like a ghost that can move in and out of situations without being noticed and some part of me finds that cathartic. Plus, my friends don't need to know every little thing about me. And honestly, they seem fine with the little I've shared.

"So, meet any women lately?" Hutch grunts as he sets the bar down.

"No," I reply because it's the truth.

When I'm home in Scotland, my accent comes out a bit. The one I got after spending half my childhood with my grandparents in a small town on an equally small island off the western coast. I had plenty of women visiting the island recently that eyed me up and I could have slept with at least three tourists, but I just wasn't in the right head space.

"Dude!" Hutch says as I miss spotting him and quickly grab the bar. He sits up and shakes his head. "Seriously, are you alright?"

"Yeah, sorry. Just lost in my thoughts," I admit in a moment of weakness.

"About a certain young woman who is living across the hall from you?" Hutch asks, waggling his eyebrows.

My glare returns and he laughs.

"No," I lie. I have been thinking about her. I can't put my finger on it, but she makes me feel...at ease, which is unusual for me. I'm not entirely sure how I feel about it.

"Right. Anyhow, I—"

"Well, looks like the gang is back together," Bray says as he and Gray walk into the room.

We do that weird bro-hug thing that I've never really understood but just accepted as a strange social norm.

"You guys almost done?" Gray asks.

"Yeah. I'm going to do my cooldown," I say, hooking my thumb toward the treadmills.

"Great. I'm going to do my run," he replies as we walk over and get on our respective treadmills. We always seem to use the same two. Bray hops on the one beside me and Hutch joins us on my other side. We all run at slightly different paces. Bray is the only true runner of us. He's done a few half-marathons. Gray runs but only a few miles. Hutch does interval training, and I just run at a steady pace for thirty minutes and then walk for another five. I glance over at Hutch. He always pushes himself even when I can tell it hurts. All three of us have to yell at him on occasion but he just keeps at it. I admire that about him.

"So, you really don't find her attractive?" Hutch asks.

"Who?" I question as I increase my cadence. Yeah, I know who, but I'll play dumb.

"Piper," he grunts as he tries to keep up with my pace.

"Yes?" a woman's voice says from behind us.

Hutch goes flying off the treadmill like a cartoon. Bray grips the handles of his to stop himself from doing the same. Gray starts laughing but doesn't miss a beat. And me, I put my feet on the sides of the treadmill and turn my head to see a gorgeous woman standing across the room from me.

She's at the door, clearly just coming in for a workout. And holy hell. She has the perfect body. I can hardly believe underneath those flowy clothes was all that toned muscle and flawless skin. Her sports bra doesn't do her breasts any justice, but they still look perfect. Her hair is tied up in a ponytail. Her shapely legs look like they should be wrapped around my waist.

Holy fuck! I need to stop ogling her. And shit, did she hear Hutch?

"Oh my God! Hutch! Are you OK?" she asks as she drops

her towel on the handle of an elliptical and runs over to check on him.

Hutch dusts off his knees and, with a little help from a nearby stair stepper, stands. "I'm good. Not the first time I've gone down and not the last."

"Damn. That looked brutal," she says as she looks him over.

He shrugs. "I've had worse."

"I didn't know everyone from the building worked out here," she says as she climbs onto the elliptical and starts her workout.

"By everyone, you mean the cool people?" Drew says from the door.

"Hey, man, you are late," Gray scolds.

Drew shrugs and gets on the last of the treadmills. "I need my beauty sleep and you fuckheads get up before the sun."

Piper snickers.

"Oh, is this Cornelia's niece?" he asks all of us.

I nod.

"I'm Piper," she says as she holds out her hand to him from across the hand bars of their machines.

"Nice to meet you. Clearly, you've met the others," he says.

"Gray, Bray, Hutch, Kasen, and you must be Cam's roommate?" she asks.

He grins. "Guilty. It's a full-time job but someone has to do it. I'm Drew, by the way."

Giggling, she picks up the pace on the machine. Everyone seems to be immersed in their workouts now and something about that is cathartic. Have I missed this routine? I guess I have.

"Does everyone from the building actually come here?" she asks.

As if on cue, Al walks in and sits down over at the leg press.

"Good morning," he says cheerfully.

"I take that as a yes," she answers herself with a laugh.

"Yeah, pretty much. Cam and Carly mostly run the trail but sometimes come here when they have free trial days. And Roxy comes here at night a few times a week for a yoga class. Jessa and Troy are not much for the workout thing. And sometimes, Al here, talks your aunt and Margie into doing weight training with him," I explain.

"The building that works out together stays together," Hutch teases. Everyone groans and Piper laughs. I glance at her reflection in the window. Fuck, she looks hot. The way her breasts move as she increases her pace. The sweat forms on the skin between her breasts. I imagine for all of two seconds how salty that sweat would taste if I licked it off her.

"How's Cornelia?" Al asks, breaking me from my very inappropriate thoughts.

"She's better now that she has her ankle pinned back together. I think she'll be back in here in a few months once we get her through some PT," Piper explains.

I can see in the window that Al is glancing at me and then back at her. Al always seems to observe everyone. He's a bit like me, except not as quiet.

"I hear you brought her your chair," he states, glancing at me as he gets up from his set on the leg press and walks over to the next machine in his circuit.

"I did. Figured she needed it more than me at the moment," I reply, wishing I had my earbuds in because I hate talking this much.

"Did she find the necklace yet?" he continues on as if we all want to talk. I love the guy, but where he could talk to anyone at any hour of the day, I prefer limited conversation, especially before nine in the morning.

"Not yet. I'm worried she lost it at the hospital or in the ambulance," Piper says with a sigh. "I know it means a lot to her, but I'm not betting on me or anyone else finding it."

"We could go down to the hospital and ask. Maybe they have a lost and found or something," I suggest and then immediately shut my mouth. Why in the hell did I offer that?

"Really? Maybe we could go after we work out?" she asks, her voice laced with so much hope I don't have the heart to say no.

"Yeah, sure," I grunt as I run.

I look into the window in front of me again and find her smiling and something about that pleases the hell out of me.

# CHAPTER SIX

Piper

"Are you sure you don't want me to stay here with you?" I ask my aunt as I swish my dress back and forth. Something about long flowy dresses with Converse shoes just makes me happy.

"No, dear. I'll be fine. I have my book, my water, and the remote. I'll call you if I need you," she says.

There's a knock on the door and I walk over and open it. Kasen is standing there holding a walkie-talkie.

"Here, Cornelia, you can use this and we'll just keep it on up there so you can talk to everyone," Kasen offers.

"Oh, that's so sweet, Kase. Thank you," my aunt says, her voice perking up at his idea.

He turns it on and does a practice "testing, one, two, three" into his.

"You press here to talk," he explains as he shows her a red button.

She tries it and they both laugh when her voice rings out from his. She pats his hand, and he gives her a big smile.

Interesting, that this broody muscle man has a sweet spot for my aunt.

"You coming up, Margie?" he asks as he walks toward her and extends his elbow.

"Of course," she states and laces her arm through his.

I wave to my aunt and follow Margie and Kasen up to the roof. I haven't been up here since arriving. It's changed a bit since I was here in high school. There's a whole seating area with a fire pit and a hot tub. The bar has been expanded and now seats four people. But there are still two tables with umbrellas, a few lounge chairs, and the greenhouse where Al grows things year-round.

"Hey, Piper, come on over and tell me what you'd like to drink," Al calls out from behind the bar. I'm not a huge drinker, so I go with a glass of chardonnay, which he pulls out of the fridge and pours into a stemless wineglass.

"Piper, it's been ages," Jessa exclaims as she walks over to me and gives me a big hug.

"How are you guys?" I ask as I get a hug from Troy next.

"Same old, just older," he quips.

"So when were you last here?" Cam asks.

"Oh, uh, well, a few times in college for an afternoon here and there, but not for a full stay since summer break when I was in high school," I explain.

"Wow, has it been that long?" Bray asks.

I nod. "I think that was my junior year summer because, after senior year, I went to Europe for the summer. So, like six years ago?"

"That explains why none of us have met you," Hutch says as he bounces a little girl on his leg. She's watching me from behind his giant arm.

"And who is this?" I ask.

"Ava," she whispers.

"Hi, Ava. I'm Piper," I say with a smile.

She grins. "Do you like to play tic-tac-toe?"

I nod. But Carly rolls her eyes. "Ava, how about you let Piper talk to everyone first and she can play with you later, OK? I bet Unca Bray will play with you."

"Set it up," Bray says with a wink, and Ava giggles and scrolls out a game board on a napkin with a marker that Al hands her.

"So has everyone moved in since then?" I ask.

"Well, Bray was here," Hutch says.

"I remember," I state.

"And I probably just had moved in then," Hutch says.

"Gray moved in two years ago and Roxy this past year. Cam and Drew moved in around the same time as Carly and Ava, so like three or so years ago," Hutch continues. It's odd getting to know people when my aunt has mentioned some of them in passing. Like Gray, I knew he was a composer because Aunt Cornelia said something about him, but I hadn't met him before being here this visit.

"I moved in four years ago," Kasen states.

"Al, how long have you owned the building?" I ask as I lean on the bar.

"Oh, gosh, I bought it around the time Edith and I got married which was nearly sixty years ago. My brother had a commercial real estate license and I thought it'd be a good investment. And it allowed Edith to have her antique store right here and it was close to my work. And now, I have all my friends living here with me, aside from a few guys I still play cards with on occasion. It's the perfect place," he says with a distant smile as if a million memories are playing in his mind like a movie.

"It does seem like a great location, especially with the dead-end street and park right here. It's unusual for a city apartment," I point out as I take a sip of wine.

"That it is. It's what drew me to it, to begin with," he explains.

"How many residents have you had over the years?" I ask.

Shrugging, he scratches his head, and I can see him mentally counting. "Oh, I reckon a few dozen. Most stay for at least five years, but a few have only stayed for a year or two."

"We moved in almost eleven years ago," my aunt pipes up from the walkie-talkie.

Al jumps and clutches his heart. "Oh my, Cornelia, you scared the daylights out of me."

She cackles. "Kasen brought them. Aren't they great? You should bring me down some wine," she insists. I want to fight her on it, but she's off her pain meds, so technically she can drink.

"Your wish is my command," Al replies with a chuckle.

"I can bring it down, Al," I offer.

He waves me off as he pours some into a stemless glass. "I got it. You enjoy yourself."

I step back and twirl around as I take in the rooftop again.

"Are you a princess?" Ava asks.

I freeze and then slowly turn back to face her. "Me?" I confirm. She nods vigorously.

I smile warmly and shake my head. "Nope. Just a normal woman."

"Oh," Ava says, her smile falling a little. "'Cause your dress twirls like a princess."

She points to the skirt of my dress. And I give it a little half twirl and her smile widens again.

"I can do that too," she says as she squirms out of Hutch's lap and takes my hand so I can twirl her. I spin her in a circle, and she giggles.

"See," she says as she points at her skirt.

"It's a very good twirly skirt," I state. I glance over to find Al watching me from the door to the stairwell.

I give him a little nod and walk Ava back to Hutch. He scoops her up and plops her back in his lap. She looks ridiculously small in his lap.

Kasen pushes a bowl of pretzels toward me. "You want some?"

I shake my head. "No, thanks."

He frowns. "Not hungry?" he asks.

"I don't really like pretzels," I say with a shrug. I mean, there's food I like less, but I'm just not a huge fan. I'd rather have something with flavor.

Kasen frowns, stands, and walks around the bar. He rifles through some cupboards and then opens the fridge. I watch with curiosity as he moves something and brings out a jar of spicy pickles. Setting them on the bar. He then pulls out some olives and celery. Before I know it, the man is making me a Bloody Mary complete with the vegetable works.

When he finishes, he pushes my mostly finished wineglass to the side and slides the alcoholic tomato juice concoction toward me. Now, I'm not a huge drinker, but this is up my alley.

I take a sip and groan. "That is really good," I say as I pop an olive in my mouth.

"Try the pickle," he demands. Normally, I don't like to be bossed around, but I can tell he means well, so I comply. My eyes widen as I chew.

"Wow. That's really good," I say as I eat some more. I look at the jar on the counter but it's not labeled.

"Al, she likes your pickles," Hutch laughs.

Al strolls over from the door where he's still silently watching us. He points to the greenhouse.

"I grow them in my garden," he says.

"Can I see?" I ask because I love a good garden.

"Sure," he replies as I pick up my drink.

I lean over the counter and kiss Kasen's cheek. "Thank you," I whisper.

I can feel him watching me as I turn and walk with Al across the rooftop to his small greenhouse.

Al explains everything he's growing. "I'm winding down my summer harvest. But I'll keep fresh herbs in here over the winter," he explains.

"It's really cool that you have this up here," I say as I look at each neatly labeled plant.

"Edith wanted a garden," he says wistfully.

"I bet she'd be happy that you're taking care of it for her," I reply as I remember his sweet wife who always made the best homemade chocolates at the holidays.

We leave the greenhouse and walk back over to the bar. I look up and find Kasen still watching me. He's talking to Hutch and putting things away. But I can see his gaze following my movements.

*You're a real mystery, Kasen. And I sort of want to get to the bottom of it and figure you out.* I should probably be applying for more jobs, but I also desperately need a distraction, and Kasen Saddler, whose last name I learned on his mailbox, is looking to be a very hot distraction.

# CHAPTER SEVEN

Kasen

The greatest part of this building is the amount of small nooks and crannies where one can be alone while also not being in their apartment. I turn to my two sea anemones.

"I'm going out. You two behave," I say to them as if they understand or even acknowledge my existence. I look at Winston, one of my clownfish. He's nuzzling Napoleon, poking his head in and out of the tentacles. Napoleon is a beadlet anemone. He's feisty. That's why I wanted him. My friends think I'm crazy for having such an obsession with a creature that seemingly doesn't even know I exist, but I find them fascinating. From the first time I went diving, I was drawn to them. They are beautiful, fascinating creatures that are misunderstood by so many. I guess I relate to them in some strange way.

"Where's Churchill?" I ask him, and as if on cue, the other clownfish appears from behind Ulysses, a snakelocks anemone. "You're in charge, Churchill."

And with that, I leave in search of the back courtyard. Everyone always hangs out on the rooftop but seldom in the back courtyard. It's not much to look at, just two benches, a butterfly bush, and a pot of seasonal flowers that Jessa switches out each season. I'm surprised when I walk outside to find an ass sticking up in the air.

I mean, it's a nice ass, but what in the hell is going on? The ass moves and I see Piper's head turn toward me.

"Uh, hey," I manage as I realize I've been caught ogling her ass and quickly look down at the ground to see what she was doing. For some reason, this woman keeps catching me off guard which is not something that happens to me often. I've literally trained to be two steps ahead of others.

She stands and brushes off her knees. "Hey," she says with a big smile that somehow starts thawing my frozen heart. Fuck, I don't like this one bit. Detached. Life is easier when I'm detached.

I look around, assessing the situation but I see nothing out of the ordinary. "What are you doing?" I finally ask as I study her unusual eyes in the sunlight, noticing that the green one actually has a fair amount of blue flecks in it.

"I came out to see if my aunt might have lost her necklace out here. She said she had sat out here right before the accident, but so far, I haven't found anything," she says with a sigh as she looks around us as if this necklace will magically appear out of thin air.

"Do you know where else she was that day?" I ask because, damn it, I did promise to help her look. And aside from a few attempts to assist, I haven't really been looking. I don't love being social, but a promise is a promise.

Piper pushes some loose hair behind her ear. "Well, she last remembers wearing it two days beforehand. She had taken it to get cleaned. Otherwise, she never takes it off," she starts.

"It's that small gold chain with the little flower that has a diamond in the center, right?" I recall.

She nods. "Yeah, my uncle gave it to her for their last anniversary. I know it means a lot to her."

Having lost so many people I love, something about this pulls at my heartstrings. Who knew that damn organ wasn't as frozen as I thought?

"OK, so can we get a list of places she went those few days?" I ask.

With another sigh, she sits down on a bench. "I wish. I already asked. But she doesn't remember. Margie said they had gotten coffee and came over here. I checked the café but didn't see anything there. Cam said she'd be on the lookout. I've checked the rooftop. And obviously the lost and found we checked at the hospital. I haven't gone by the fire station where the ambulance came from yet. I should probably do that," she says.

"Do you know if it was the one around the corner?" I ask.

She nods. "Yes, that's what the medical report she got says. Do you know where it is?"

"Yes. Come on, it's not far and I was just wanting some fresh air," I state.

"Are you sure? I don't want to intrude on your time," she says as she stands. Her foot slips on some moss on a paver and she starts to fall backward. I reach out, grabbing her, and pulling her against me. Her hands fly to my chest as she steadies herself.

For reasons I'm not ready to explore, I don't let go right away.

"You alright, there?" I ask as I look into those multicolored eyes that are wide with surprise.

She nods but doesn't speak.

"Are you guys going to kiss?" Ava's voice rings out from above us.

We both look up to find her leaning out a window.

"Ava, get inside. It's dangerous to lean out of the window," I scold.

"Mr. Gray said the same thing the other day," she says as if grownups are idiots.

"Ava," I growl.

She giggles and slides back inside her apartment.

Piper clears her throat and I slowly release her.

"She's a funny kid, huh?" Piper says, her cheeks are bright pink and I wonder if she's embarrassed to have been caught with me in such a position.

"That she is," I agree as I follow her out to the front where I turn right and she walks alongside me.

"So, I heard you were helping your grandmother recently," she starts as we begin walking toward the fire station.

I nod.

"Is she doing better?" she asks.

I nod.

"You don't say much, do you?" she questions.

I shrug. "I guess not."

I glance over to find her pursing her lips as if considering this fact about me.

"Where did you grow up?"

"Are we playing twenty questions?" I ask.

"Sure," she replies, a grin spreading across her face.

I groan and she giggles. "Oh, come on, indulge me. I mean, it's not like I live here. You probably won't see me again for months," she explains. "Or more, depending on if I ever find a job and it's not around here."

"You're looking for a job?" I ask.

"Yeah. I'm trying to figure that whole career thing out," she says and then lowers her voice to a whisper. "It's not going very well."

I fight a laugh because I remember being in those same

shoes years ago when I decided just to join the military instead of going to college or getting a job. "I see."

"So?"

"So?" I repeat.

"Where did you grow up?" she repeats her question. This woman is frustrating as fuck. I can tell she isn't going to relent, so I figure what the hell?

"Well, when I was a wee lad, I lived in Maine with my parents. And then when I was a teenager, I went to live with my grandparents in Scotland," I explain.

I look back to see her grinning again.

"What?" I ask as I try to figure out what I said that was so funny.

"Wee lad," she repeats my words with a laugh. "That explains why I sometimes hear a faint accent when you speak."

She's not wrong. I tend to have my Scottish accent pop out when I drink or when my guard is down. My father's accent remained strong until his final day and then living on a remote Scottish island for four years had me acquiring a bit of one. I did my best to cover it up when I decided to go back to the States and join the military.

"I suppose so," I say as we reach the end of the block and I turn us right.

"So, you must be close to your grandmother," she says, her elbow brushing my arm. I watch her out of the corner of my eye. She's looking at me and not watching where she is going.

"Watch your step, curious cat," I tease.

She looks back down in time to avoid a planter along the edge of the sidewalk. "I guess what they say about curiosity killing the cat is true, huh?" she says with a slight laugh, keeping her eyes ahead.

"How long were you in the military?" she asks.

I raise an eyebrow because I never told her I was in the military.

"I saw your dog tags on the wall of your living room when you opened your door the other day," she explains and I'm instantly impressed by her attention to such a small detail.

But I still hate all the questioning. This is why I don't date. So many questions. So many things I don't want to remember. I've spent my whole life running from my memories. And so far, I've managed to keep away from them.

"Five years," I say, remembering when a beachside bomb changed my life. It gave me a concussion, a nasty scar on my forehead, and some hearing damage. But it was the stitches on my trigger finger that kept me from going back into the field. I still don't feel everything on that finger, but I have most of my mobility back.

I got honorably discharged and then I went back to school and got my degree in cybersecurity. I managed to snag an internship with a government contractor my senior year and I've been working with them and now as a private consultant for the past three years.

"And now you do computer stuff?" she asks.

"Cybersecurity," I correct.

"That sounds intense," she states as she stops to pet a dog that a man is walking.

We continue on our way.

"What do you want to do?" I ask, deciding to deflect her questioning with one of my own.

She's quiet for a few steps. "I don't know. That's what I'm trying to figure out."

"You like painting and drawing and you're good at it. Can't you do that?" I ask as I remember watching her paint. It's odd how soothing it was to watch.

"I could, but it's hard to get started. Not a lot of money and I need to pay my bills," she explains with a sad smile.

"So what are you going to do?" I inquire because I hate to see talent wasted.

Shrugging, she looks away and I wonder what she's thinking.

"I guess get a normal job for now," she says in a distant voice. I can tell she's conflicted. Even though I'm nearly a decade older than her, I remember starting out as an adult and how hard it was. I made a rash decision to join the Navy and it changed the course of my entire life, both for bad and good.

"Well, you can still freelance, right?"

"I suppose so," she says as we round the last corner and I point to the fire station.

Her face returns to its happy norm as she grabs my hand. "Come on, let's go see if they have it," she says excitedly.

For some reason, her innocent happiness makes *me* happy, a feeling I haven't experienced in a while, at least not like this. I honestly don't know how to respond to her. Unlike so many women I interact with, she hasn't once indicated she wants anything sexual from me. She doesn't spend the entire conversation ogling me, and she wants to talk, really talk. She's a breath of fresh air and it unnerves me a bit. I've never been caught off guard by a woman in all my life. And I don't know what to make of it, but I do know I like spending time with her. So as we walk inside the fire station, a small part of me hopes we don't find the necklace today, because then I'll have an excuse to spend more time with her.

# CHAPTER EIGHT

Piper

The firehouse was another dead end, but I did have a nice lunch with Kasen where I attempted to pry more information from him. Kasen is like a vault. And every time I got even the smallest nugget of information, I felt that much closer to cracking the vault open. I don't mind that he's quiet, but I also wish he would confide in me. I can't help but feel he has so many things he should talk about.

I've decided after sorting Aunt Cornelia out this morning, I'm going to paint.

"Whatcha doin'?" a voice says from my right.

I jump a little and clutch my chest until I see Hutch in camo standing beside a tree.

"Hutch?" I ask as I take in his unusual appearance.

"Yep, just watching and waiting," he says.

I look around. The sun just came up and it's quiet. Occasionally a jogger runs on the trail behind me, but otherwise, I've been enjoying the peace.

"Uh, for what?" I ask, looking around.

"The Guardian of Hearts Lane Park, of course," he says as if that should make sense to me.

"Huh?"

He motions to the bench where I'm sitting. "Every morning, there are flowers there with a note. It almost always says, *If you found these flowers, then the universe wants you to feel loved. Take them home and enjoy them. XOXO, The Guardian of Hearts Lane Park*," he says as if this is common knowledge.

"Oh, I've seen them," I say, recalling when I found them a few days ago and then once when I visited in high school.

"Well, it's been happening for years, and I want to know who it is. I mean, we all do," Hutch says.

"A mystery, huh?"

He nods. "I'm going to figure it out someday."

"Cool," I reply because I'm not sure why this grown-ass man wants to solve a flower mystery so badly. But whatever floats his boat.

"Nice painting," he says while admiring the lily pads I've painted.

"Thanks, I'm trying to practice," I explain as I begin working on a small frog sitting on the lily pad. "So, do you like to come out here every morning to look?"

"Sometimes before or after the gym. Kasen and I go to the gym at least three times a week," he says.

"Yeah, I need to go back again. I signed up for a month's trial membership while I'm visiting," I explain.

"It's a good gym. Not a ton of bells and whistles but it's close by," he says casually.

"So, you and Kasen are good friends, then?" I'm not sure why I ask. It's none of my business but I keep thinking about Kasen, especially since we went to the fire station. Fine, I'm curious about this seemingly grumpy, private, hot-as-fuck man. I think it's because he's different from every guy I've been on a date with. He's mysterious but also kind and he marches to his own beat, which I identify with.

"Yeah. He's a good person. He's helped me a lot over the past few years, including being my lifting partner at the gym, but also just...being a friend." Hutch looks over at me and I stop painting. "I know he's kind of quiet and all, but he really is a great person."

"Who's a great person?"

We both turn and see Al standing there.

"Oh, uh, Kasen," Hutch says.

"Morning, Mr. Al," I say to him as I turn a bit to face him.

"Off on my morning walk. What are you two up to?" he asks, looking Hutch up and down, clearly wondering why Hutch is in camo just as I am.

"Just waiting for the flowers to arrive," Hutch explains as he pats the bench.

Al nods and looks at me. "Nice painting, Piper. You have real talent."

I blush. "Thank you. I'm working on it."

"Hey, would you mind painting some of my pots in the greenhouse?" he asks.

"Oh, sure. I can do that," I say, trying not to sound too excited. I've never had anyone ask me to paint anything.

"Great. I'll be up there later, come by when you have a moment," he says as he waves and continues on with his walk.

The colorful sunrise is starting to fade into a sunny day, so I start packing up my art supplies. I'll grab some coffee and muffins and head back up to help my aunt get sorted for the morning. She always likes to get up and watch some television before she eats and gets a sponge bath.

"Well, I'm off to get some coffee and check in on my aunt. I guess..." I look around. "Enjoy your stakeout?"

He chuckles. "I'll come with you. I could use something to eat. This will all be here again tomorrow."

I finish packing up and we head over to the café. "So, how often do you..." I trail off as I motion to the bench. I freeze and my mouth drops open. Sitting on the bench are flowers.

"For fuck's sake," Hutch mutters under his breath.

I laugh. "Sorry, I probably messed that up for you."

He waves me off. "No, that always happens. As soon as I'm distracted...BAM! They just appear."

"Maybe it's magic," I tease.

"Right," he grumbles as he holds open the café door.

"Good morning," Cam says as she finishes ringing up a customer.

"Hey, can I get three black coffees with caramel syrup and three blueberry muffins?" I ask.

"Sure." Cam looks at Hutch.

"The usual," he says.

"OK," she says as she gets busy with the order.

"How's Cornelia doing?" Cam asks while bagging up the muffins.

"Good. Later this week, she'll be getting the cast off and then she can shower," I answer as I take the bag of muffins and tap my credit card on her machine.

"That's great news. Hopefully, she's back to normal soon. And, Hutch, here's your small dirty chai tea latte with regular milk and two shots of espresso."

He tosses some cash down on the counter.

"Thanks, Cam," he says as he walks toward the door and holds it for me. I grab the tray of lattes and follow him out.

"See ya, Cam," I call out and she waves back as she helps another customer.

We walk in silence until I get to the elevator. "It was nice talking," I say because it was nice. It's been great talking to everyone here. They are all so kind. I've never really felt part of a community, but only a week into being here and I feel like everyone has accepted me into their inner circle.

"It was. Keep painting. You got something special there," he says as he takes the stairs, leaving me to take the elevator alone. My mind goes back to what he said about Kasen being a good person. I don't disagree. I just wish I could get him to open up a bit more.

———

"Mr. Al!" I call out as I step out onto the rooftop. It's been an hour, and when I texted Al, he said he was already up here.

"In here, Piper," he answers from the greenhouse.

I walk over and stop in my tracks when I see Kasen. It's not just Kasen being here that has me freezing. Nope. It would be the fact that Kasen's not wearing a shirt. He's hard at work trying to secure something to a bolt in the green-house ceiling. And holy hell! I knew he was in good shape from seeing him at the gym, but...do humans actually look like that? He's got a full abdomen of muscles and his chest is...wow, just wow.

I realize I'm gawking and I quickly close my mouth.

"Oh, hey there," I say to Kasen as I watch him work. Stepping inside the greenhouse, I now understand why he's shirtless. It's really hot in here, and surprisingly large. From the outside, it doesn't look huge but it's big enough for a large potting table, two large shelves, and several plant stands. There is a large metal bin-like tub at the far end that's acting as some kind of planter. And I watch as Kasen hangs some chain from the bolt and clips on a hanging planter.

"There," he says as he steps down from a small ladder.

"These are the pots," Al says as he points to three large terra-cotta pots on the table.

"Oh, OK. Can I take them outside to paint?" I ask.

"I suppose, but any chance you can paint them here." He motions to the table. "Just in case you get paint anywhere," he adds and then looks to Kasen. "Kasen is helping me add some hanging planters in here. It'll double the amount of plants I can grow over the winter.

"That's nice," I say warmly as I lift the first pot, which is surprisingly heavy.

"Here, let me," Kasen says as he steps behind me and easily lifts the pot. I point to the far side of the table and he sets it down. But I'm no longer paying attention to the pot because right now, I'm encased by Kasen. His scent fills my nostrils. His warmth permeates through my top. His hot breath tickles my ear. A part of me that I have continually suppressed suddenly activates as if every single light in a car's dashboard has come on at once. And a very startling thought enters my brain.

I want Kasen. I want Kasen to touch me and not in a friend way. Oh shit! I'm so fucked.

# CHAPTER NINE

Kasen

I pound my fist on my desk. Damn, this hacker is good. I've been trying to plug holes in the firewall for this company for hours and somehow the hacker we hired to break through my firewall keeps finding a weakness in my code. The question is: Where's my mistake?

I push back from the desk and decide I need a break. I walk into my living room and stop in my tracks.

Water. Shit, there's water everywhere.

Oh no, I rush over to my fish tank. I see dripping from the corner. How in the hell did it spring a leak? The water level is lower, but the leak is slow. It must have been going on for a while. I knew I should have upgraded tanks when I got home. Two years ago this leaked and I managed to patch it with Troy's help. Looks like he's about to assist again.

I pull out my phone and text him.

Me: So, I may have sprung another leak.

Troy: Damn, same place?

I look over at the tank to confirm.

Me: I think so.

Troy: Be right down.

Hanging up, I go to the door and unlock. I open it, waiting for Troy. The door across the hall flies open and Piper steps out and then screeches.

"Oh my God! You scared the crap out of me," she says, clutching her chest.

"Sorry, waiting on Troy to fix my tank," I explain as I motion into the living room. I really ought to mop up that water.

"Your fish tank?" she asks as she sticks her head into my apartment and then looks up at me. "Do you have towels? You should mop up that water before it ruins your floor."

"I was just thinking that," I state. "Do you mind waiting here for Troy? He's coming down to help me fix it."

"Sure," she says as she leans on the door, holding it open. I rush back inside and grab a handful of towels from my linen closet. I place them on the floor, sopping up the water.

"Where's the leak?" Troy's voice booms from the hallway as he walks inside and kneels to examine where I'm pointing.

"Same as last time, maybe a little higher?" I say as I too kneel down and take a look.

"Looks like it. Maybe we weakened the joint when we put that epoxy in there. Let's do the whole joint this time," he suggests.

I nod and we get to work.

"Can I help with anything?" Piper asks from the door.

I wave her over. "You can. Mind grabbing more towels?"

She nods and heads in the direction where I'm pointing. I look at my sea creature. "Hang in there, guys. We're going to get this all fixed up for you," I assure them.

Troy groans. "Kid, you need to find a woman or a pet you can actually hold. Might I recommend the woman option?"

I glare at him and then realize Piper is standing next to me holding out the towels.

"Thank you," I say and place them on the ground. It takes Troy and me a few minutes to concoct a plan and then another few minutes for him to get the materials, which we fortunately had from the last time.

Piper insists on staying and assisting. Like the stereotype of a child helping their father with a plumbing issue by handing them tools, Piper quietly sits by and hands us materials when we ask for them. She doesn't say much, just watches.

It takes the better part of an hour, but eventually, we fix the leak after I had to put up a barrier in the tank to keep the water from the corner.

"Try to keep it dry for at least twenty-four hours," Troy reminds me.

"Yeah. Got it," I mutter. "Thanks again."

He claps me on my back, and I fight the feeling that brings to me. I keep those feelings buried so deep that I'd need an excavator to bring them to the surface. But every so often, some emotions start to fester and tunnel up through the thick layers I've created.

"See ya, Piper," Troy says with a tip of his baseball cap.

"Bye, Troy," she says, offering him a little wave. We're left standing there and staring at my fish and sea anemones.

"So...sea anemones, huh?" she states as she stares at them.

"Yep." She looks at me and then back at them.

I point to each one. "That's Napoleon. He's a beadlet anemone. He's feisty. And that's Winston, he lives inside," I say as I point to the little clownfish. "And that is Ulysses. He's a snakelocks anemone, and Churchill lives inside him," I add.

"Wow...interesting choice of names," she says. "And how is an anemone feisty?"

I laugh. "They just are. It's the species."

"Uh-huh," she murmurs. "Well, they're pretty."

"Of course they are. My children are gorgeous," I say in mock horror.

Piper starts giggling and then full-on snorts while laughing. "I'm sorry," she manages after a minute. "I just...you are too much. Who knew you were capable of such affection with sea creatures?"

I shrug.

"Hey, I'm sorry. I didn't mean to hurt your feelings. It's just...I guess I never thought of fish and such having feelings or being gorgeous." She pauses and leans in to look more closely at my pets. "I mean, I guess they are. Have you seen any in the wild?"

I nod. "That's where my fascination started."

"Did you dive a lot growing up?" she asks.

"I learned as a kid, but then I was in the Navy and, well, I spent a lot of time in the water," I explain.

"You must be a really good swimmer. I suck at it. But I do like to snorkel as long as I can stand up. I've gone a few times when I've been on vacations," she says and something about that makes me sad for her.

"You never learned to swim?" I ask.

Shaking her head, she turns back to me. "No. My mom made me take some lessons, but I was little and afraid. I can doggie paddle a bit but I only go in water where I can reach the bottom."

"I think we should fix that. I can give you a lesson at the gym. I mean, the pool isn't great, but it'd work," I offer.

She purses her lips and cocks her head to the side. "Maybe."

"What? Don't trust me?" I tease.

She rolls her eyes. "I don't know you that well."

And with that simple sentence, I feel closer to her than I

have to anyone in a long time. Her past has taught her not to trust, just like mine.

"Were you going somewhere...I mean, before you helped me here?"

"Just to get some coffee. I should probably get back and check on my aunt," she says.

"You want to eat with me? I'm ordering some delivery. I don't want to leave the tank until I know the patch is holding," I explain.

She's silent for a long beat and I begin to wonder if she doesn't want to hang out with me, but then she speaks. "Sure. I just need to get Aunt Cornelia settled. Give me thirty minutes."

"OK," I reply as I walk her to the door. "I'll leave it unlocked. Come back over when you're ready."

With a slight nod, she leaves and I go about drying the floor a little more and placing my now-drenched towels in the washer. By the time I finish, she's back.

"Italian or Italian?" I ask.

"Oh, that's a tough choice. Uh, I'm going to have to go with...Italian," she replies with a grin.

I pat the stool next to mine at my kitchen counter and she sits. We scroll through a few menus and find one she likes, and I order us food.

"Drink?" I ask.

"Sure." She watches me as I walk around my counter and show her what I have. "I have whiskey, gin, beer, water, and... orange juice," I rattle off as I close my refrigerator door.

"Water is fine," she says. I pour myself a whiskey because, after that tank catastrophe, I need it.

"Is that Scottish whiskey?" she asks.

I push the glass toward her. "It is. I got some when I was helping my grandmother out," I explain. She studies it for a beat and then takes a small sip.

I watch her roll the liquid around her mouth and something about that simple action makes my pulse pick up a beat. How can tasting whiskey be sexy?

"It's actually not bad," she admits with a shrug.

"Not bad? That is a ninety-pound bottle of whiskey. It's the best," I chastise.

"Fine. It's great. I'll have a glass," she says dryly.

"Are you fucking with me? Or do you actually want some?"

She laughs. "I do want some."

"Now we're talking," I say as I grab a glass and pour her a finger of whiskey. We clink glasses.

"To sea anemones," she says with a wink.

"To neighborly visitors," I reply. Only watching her drink makes me want to do more than neighborly things to her.

# CHAPTER TEN



Piper

"And then I used the tways in the high school cafeteria and we swent sledding," I slur.

"On the trays?" Kasen confirms.

I nod enthusiastically, holding out my hands to show how large they were.

He laughs. "Did you get caught?"

I shake my head and immediately regret it because everything blurs. "Whoa," I whisper.

Kasen takes my third glass of whiskey and drinks the rest.

"That's enough of that, lightweight," he teases.

I look at the clock on his microwave. "Oh no. I need to chweck on Aunt Cornelia," I say, knowing that I'm slurring and feeling too tired to care.

"Come here," Kasen says as he gets off his stool and holds out a hand. I place mine in his.

"You have bwig hands," I think, but when he laughs, I realize I said that out loud.

"And you have small hands. Now come sit. I'm going to check on her for you. I'll be right back," he promises as he squeezes my hand, and when he releases it, I immediately wish he was holding it again. I curl up on his oversized leather sofa and pull a soft blanket over me. It smells like Kasen, all woodsy and clean. In the warmth of the blanket, I suddenly wish it was Kasen wrapped around me, keeping me warm. I burrow deeper and start to fall asleep. My eyelids grow heavy and the last thing I remember is hearing the gurgling of the device in the fish tank that puts air in the water.

———

I wake with a start. I'm much warmer than before and the blanket is heavy, like really, really heavy. I go to move but I can't. My eyes pry open and I immediately close them. Way too much light and my head is pounding. What time is it?

I slowly open my eyes again and look around. And that's when I find the source of the warmth and my inability to move.

Kasen.

He's fallen asleep next to me; he's using my hip as a pillow. His arms are wrapped around my middle. His breaths come slow and steady. I take a moment to look at him. He's gorgeous in a rugged sort of way. His dark hair is messy and he has a bit of a beard. The faint scar above his right eye intrigues me. I wonder when or where he got it. Was it when he was in the Navy?

His hands are large, which I already knew, but they seem bigger now that he's wrapped around me. I wonder what those hands would feel like if they touched my skin beneath my T-shirt.

I contemplate how I can extricate myself from him, but

then his eyelids flutter open. He stares at me for a few seconds. Neither of us speaks.

"I think we fell asleep," he says groggily as he slowly gets up.

"Yeah. What time is it?" I had come over in the afternoon, we had dinner, I drank way too much, and then I remember him sitting me down here and after that...well, I guess I fell asleep.

"Oh, shit!" I say as I get up with a start. "Aunt Cornelia!" I race to the door but Kasen's faster and his giant hand holds it shut. "Kasen, I got to go."

His body is flush with mine, pressing me to the door. I shiver from the contact.

"I already helped her. I went over again this morning. I must have dozed off afterward. She's fine, Piper. I promise," he says quietly against the shell of my ear. His hot breath has my skin prickling.

I swallow, giving myself a moment to collect my thoughts. "Oh, uh, thank you," I manage. I sway a little, feeling light-headed.

"Let's get you a breakfast sandwich and coffee," he suggests. "It'll help with the hangover."

"I'm not really very hungry," I reply as waves of nausea come over me. I am never drinking again.

His finger brushes along my arm. "Don't be such an escape artist. Let me get you breakfast and then we can both get on with our days, OK?"

"Escape artist? I'm hardly escaping. I just need to check on my aunt," I protest.

"And I'm telling you I just did two hours ago and she's fine. We can get them breakfast too," he offers. "Please let me get you breakfast for helping with the tank."

"You got me dinner," I retort.

"And that was for helping with the water on the floor," he

states. Damn, he's good at arguing and I'm too tired to protest.

"Fine," I say like a petulant child.

Kasen grabs his key and we walk over to the café.

"You two look wrecked," Cam says with a laugh. "I think we will need some serious coffees today." She gives me a look and I nod.

"On it."

"And two breakfast sandwiches, two muffins, and lattes for Cornelia and Margie," Kasen adds.

I lean on the counter and look back at the apartment building. "Does someone have a black cat?" I ask.

Kasen and Cam both look over.

Kasen groans. "It's Licorice. She probably wants in the store. She must have escaped Gray's apartment."

"He has a cat?"

They nod in unison.

"I'm going to grab it," I announce as I walk over to the bookshop door where the cat is sitting and waiting.

"Hey, little one You waiting for the store to open?" I ask it.

"Meow!" it replies as it looks up at me with big green eyes.

"You're very pretty," I say, leaning down and letting it smell my hand before I scoop it up in my arms. I stroke its soft fur and its eyes drift closed. It starts purring and I smile down at it.

"Oh, there she is. Licorice!" Roxy scolds and I hand the cat to her after she opens the door.

"I swear that cat is going to give up all nine lives before she even reaches nine years old." She pauses and looks at me. "Long night?"

"You have no idea," I reply, following her inside while she opens the store. I sit in a big comfy chair by the front windows.

She looks over at the café and back at me. "Kasen, huh?"

I blush. "Oh, no. It's not like that. I was helping him with his fish tank and then we had dinner, and I drank way too much whiskey and passed out on his sofa," I explain.

"I mean. Kasen is hot," Roxy says.

"I suppose so. I just...hadn't really thought about that," I lie. She gives me a pointed look.

"Fine, yes, he's hot."

She sits down in the chair next to me and Licorice rubs against her legs. "I think he's interested in you."

"You do?"

She nods. "Yeah. He keeps glancing over here every three seconds. I've never seen him do that. Not that I know him super well yet, but Gray said he thought maybe he liked you. And I agree."

"You think Kasen likes me?" I ask, pointing to my chest. And since when did *I* become the focus of gossip? No one ever pays attention to *me*.

"Yes. Wait. Do you already have a boyfriend?" she asks. "Or a girlfriend?"

I shake my head as my whole face turns red.

"I'm sorry. I didn't mean to embarrass you." She gives me a sympathetic look.

"It's not that. I just...I've never had a boyfriend," I whisper as if someone might hear it.

"Like, ever?" she asks with a raised eyebrow.

I shake my head and bite my bottom lip.

"Wow. OK. Well, there's nothing wrong with that," she says. "I mean, lots of women haven't had boyfriends."

I give her a pointed look. "I hardly think that's the case. I just...my parents' separation made having friends hard and then I was always in art programs and busy in high school. And in college, I just never got the hang of the dating thing." *Why am I telling her all of this?*

"You've never dated?" a voice says from the doorway as the bell rings.

It's Al. Great, just great. Now, everyone can *really* gossip about me.

Al looks to Roxy. "I think we need to remedy that."

Wonderful. Now a senior citizen is trying to fix my dry spell. *If you've never had sex, is it still a dry spell?* Could my life get any more embarrassing?

"Remedy what?" Kasen says from behind Al.

Yes, yes my life can get more embarrassing.

"Oh, nothing. Just trying to set our Piper up on a date," Al announces. I look down at the floor, hoping a hole will open up and swallow me because there is no way I can look Kasen in the eyes ever again.

"A date, huh?" Kasen repeats.

"Yep. She's never had a proper one. Sounds like she could use some practice," Roxy says and gives Kasen a look.

"I mean, I've been on a few dates," I interject, not wanting it to seem like I have lived under a rock or something.

"Do you want dating practice?" Kasen asks me and now I'm really hoping a portal to another dimension will open or an alternate universe. Something? Anything?

"Guys, it's fine. Really. I should be focusing on Aunt Cornelia," I insist.

"I can take you out," Kasen offers. I freeze as I start to stand and then slowly realize I look crazy and finish standing.

"It's OK. You are so busy. You don't have to do that," I state.

"I think Kasen would be a great man to take you out on a date so you can practice," Al says with a big smile.

"What do you say?" Kasen adds.

I'm clearly not escaping this. "Fine. One practice date," I say because I just want to get this mortification over with.

"Who's going on a practice date?" Drew says from behind Kasen. For the love of God! Will this embarrassment ever end?

"We are," Kasen announces as he uses his free hand to point at me.

Drew looks from Kasen to me. "Girl, Kasen is going to ruin you for real dates, but hey, it's your dating funeral. Cheerio, lads and lasses," Drew says with a wave as he walks over to the café.

Kasen groans.

"Well, I'm off for my walk. You kids have fun on your date. I can't wait to hear all about it," Al says cheerily.

"I gotta open the register. Feel free to eat here," Roxy suggests as she leaves me standing in front of Kasen who is holding a tray of drinks and a bag of food.

"Come on, let's go eat and we can plan this pretend date," Kasen says as he pushes the door open with his perfectly tight ass.

My face remains red the entire elevator ride upstairs. This is definitely going to kill me. How am I supposed to go on a practice date with this man that I have a crush on? I'm so screwed.

# CHAPTER ELEVEN

Kasen

It only takes one minute and twenty-seven seconds, give or take, to determine that Piper really doesn't know much about dating. She can quite literally count all the dates she's been on with her fingers and toes.

I swear with each of my questions her face turns a darker shade of pink.

"So, you really haven't dated much," I state, a little shocked.

Her face darkens again into an almost red hue. She nods and keeps her eyes on her feet. I reach out and slowly push her face up with my forefinger. Eventually, her eyes meet mine.

"There's nothing to be ashamed about or embarrassed about, little escape artist. It just seems to be that you've managed to escape romance altogether. But we're going to work on that and find you the romance you deserve," I assure her. I shouldn't be around this woman. She's too damned tempting. But I can't let some jackass ruin her heart because she is unsure of herself on a date. I can do this. I can help her. And then she'll leave and I can move on with life knowing I did something good.

"I have a college degree. I'm a full-grown woman and don't know the first thing about dating. It's so embarrassing," she whispers as if someone else will hear her. I drop my finger.

"First, you said you've technically been on twelve dates. Three with one guy, two with three others, and one with three others. So, you have dated. But you also said that ten of those dates were in high school with boys you had class with, so children. No offense, but you were all not experienced, so of course they sucked at dating too. And it sounds like the two college dates were with jackasses who only wanted one thing."

She looks at me confused for a second and then that pink color returns. Damn, she's innocent. I'd ruin her for sure. Time to turn on the big-brother vibe. I'm always happy to play that card with any of women in the building—since they are the only women I see on the regular.

"Are you sure you want to do this?" she asks.

"Yes," I assure her.

She puts her hands on her hips and gives me a sassy look. "What are your credentials?"

I nearly choke on my saliva. "Are you questioning my experience?" I growl.

"I mean. I laid my dating life, or lack thereof, out on the table. It's your turn. Quid pro quo," she challenges, her singular eyebrow over her green eye moving higher on her forehead.

"Fine. My first kiss was when I was thirteen. I had two long-term girlfriends in high school and probably went out on a dozen or so dates with other girls. I went on a few dates during my time in the Navy, but honestly, it was more one-night stands when I had leave. Then in college, I had a long-term girlfriend for a year, the longest girlfriend. After that, I've had a string of dates, but mostly I kept a hook-up buddy for emergencies," I state matter-of-factly.

"For emergencies?" she asks.

"Yep." I don't elaborate. I honestly haven't spoken to that woman in over three months, right before I left on what was supposed to be a work trip but turned into nearly three months of staying with my grandmother.

She drops her hands from her hips. "Dinner and maybe a movie," she says.

"OK. I can do that. When?"

"Tomorrow?" she asks.

I have a standing online game tomorrow. Shit. I don't want to tell the boys what I'm doing. Then I remember Roxy and Al heard our conversation. Would they tell the others?

"How about the day after tomorrow? I have a previous commitment tomorrow," I offer, deciding I should keep my standing game even if they do find out.

She looks at me with curiosity and then her face falls. Damn it.

"Not that. It's a game with friends," I admit.

"Oh, OK. That works," she says. She goes to leave and looks back at me. "What should I wear?"

"Whatever you'll be comfortable in. But it'll be a nicer restaurant, not a local bar," I say as I decide on the location.

"What does that even mean?" she protests.

"It means, no jeans and T-shirts, but dresses, pants, nicer tops are fine, nothing too fancy. We aren't going to prom," I try to explain.

"What are you wearing?" she asks. Now I'm getting exasperated.

"Black pants, gray sweater," I say with a clenched jaw.

Her lips twitch and then she manages to say, "OK, I'll see you at...?"

"I'll pick you up at six," I state.

"Oh, uh, can I just come over here? I don't want my aunt knowing," she says.

"What about Al and Roxy?" I ask because they clearly know.

"I'll tell them to keep it quiet," she says.

"Good luck with that," I tease and she groans.

"Fine, pick me up at six. But I'm telling them we are just going out as friends," she grumbles.

"Fine," I reply as she leaves me standing there wondering what I just agreed to.

———

"You agreed to do what?" Bray asks as we play the game. Bray, when he's not working, joins me online and so does Hutch. Gray and Drew tend to not play but they will consume a drink and chat with us. I specifically made a setup at my place where we can connect all our computers separately and still hang out.

"I agreed to a practice date. I mean, shit, someone needs to teach her," I huff, suddenly feeling overprotective of Piper.

"What the fuck do you know about romance?" Hutch says with a laugh.

I glare at him and he just keeps laughing.

"Fuck you," I curse.

"Whatever, but seriously what if she, like, falls for you and shit. You can't just break her heart," he says, his laughter dying.

"I won't. I'm not that heartless," I protest.

Everyone stops talking and I feel their eyes on me. I look up from the game. "What?"

"I mean, you were trained to kill people," Bray points out.

"That's different. That was the military," I state, trying to keep myself from remembering everything I did during that time period.

"It's just...she's, like, real sweet. And also, can't anyone in this building just have a normal relationship instead of fake dating or practice dating or whatever?" Drew says from my kitchen where he's mixing drinks. Gray is sitting at my counter and he looks at me for a long moment.

"What?" I ask as I make eye contact with him.

"Do you like her?" he questions.

Oh, fuck no. I'm not playing that game.

"I don't like women. I fuck women and that's it. No more relationships. I don't have time for that shit," I say, but the words seem hollow because deep down, I know that's not true.

"I think Allison really fucked you up," Bray states, his eyes staying focused on our game. "On your right."

I put my head back in the game and don't answer him. He's not wrong. My last ex did fuck me up. I was dealing with a lot of PTSD issues post my injury while serving. She eventually said I was too fucked up from everything in my past and she needed someone who wasn't a lifelong fixer-upper project.

"Doesn't matter," I mutter.

"It does. You deserve better," Bray says.

"He's right," Hutch agrees. "I know you got this tough-military, mysterious-cybersecurity, gym-rat thing going on"—he motions to my body—"but I'm pretty sure beneath your candied hard shell, you are all gooey on the inside."

"Dude, that was some poetic shit," Drew teases.

Hutch glares at him. "I'm not a Longfellow, OK? But you know what I mean."

"Kase, just don't rule out making yourself happy. You're allowed to be happy," Drew says.

"Speaking of happy, where's Vito?" I ask, deciding we need to end this conversation about my nonexistent love life.

"He is back in Italy," Drew says.

We all pause and look over at him.

"Come on, guys. We all knew that the Italian Stallion was going to have to return to his mother country after he finished his graduate program," Drew says trying to be light-hearted but I see right through that shit.

"Drew, man, I'm sorry. Do you think you could go see him?" I ask, feeling bad for my friend. He'd been dating that guy for almost eight months.

"Nah. I live here. He lives on the other side of the world. We had great times, but it's over," Drew states. He turns to Hutch.

"What about Jocelyn?" he asks.

Hutch coughs. "What? What about her?"

"I see the way you two are always talking. What's going on there?" he presses.

"Nothing. She's just nice and we chat sometimes. Am I not allowed to be friends with girls?" he says defensively.

"You are, but Jocelyn is a very pretty girl," Bray states.

"Like you have room to talk. You practically are married to Carly and yet you won't just seal the deal. Seriously, I could cut the sexual tension between you two with a knife," Hutch says as we all look at Bray.

Bray groans. "We all know that Carly is like my sister. Nothing is going to happen there. We all know about her past." The room is quiet again. Carly's ex was a monster, and we all know it.

The room's energy turns back to me.

"So, you need dating advice? I could call Roxy," Gray says with a grin. I throw a pillow at him and he laughs.

"Fuck you very much," I mutter.

"Hey, don't knock those romance books she sells until you try them. My sex life has never been so good," Gray states.

"We are all going to pretend we didn't hear that," Drew says as he pours him another drink. I spend the rest of the game wondering if Gray has a point. Maybe I do need to brush up on my skills.

# CHAPTER TWELVE

Piper

Why am I nervous? I look at myself in the bathroom mirror for the tenth time in as many minutes. I look fine. I feel like this is my first date. Sighing, I open the door because no more amount of prepping can have me relaxing over this practice dating thing. What was I thinking?

"You look lovely," Margie says as she walks down the hallway. Margie always appears calm as a cucumber. I wish I had a fraction of her ability to remain unfazed by life.

"Thank you," I reply as I walk into the living room. Aunt Cornelia is knitting in the chair Kasen brought her. I swear between her and Margie knitting and crocheting, they could start a clothing line. A cup of tea sits on the side table and some horrible reality show about couples meeting on a tropical island plays in the background.

"So, you're seeing a movie with Kasen?" she asks, her eyebrow rises but she doesn't look up at me. Instead, she keeps her focus on the two sticks working back and forth in her hands. I make a mental note that I should have her teach me how to knit. She taught me to crochet when I was a kid, so knitting ought to be easy enough.

"Yep. Hey, can you teach me how to knit?" I ask.

She stops and looks up at me. "I suppose so. We can have a lesson tomorrow."

I smile and she motions for me to come over to her. I walk up beside her chair and she looks up at me. For a long second, I think she's going to say something important, a piece of grandmotherly advice. But boy am I wrong.

"There are condoms in my nightstand drawer. Take three. Slash that. Take five. Kasen seems...prolific," she states and then waves me off to her room.

I half cough and half laugh. "I...uh, no. That's not happening. It's just a movie and some food."

She eyes me suspiciously. "Fine, but at least take one."

She reaches into the pocket of her robe and pulls out a small foil packet and my eyes nearly bulge out of my head.

"Aunt Cornelia! Why in the hell do you have a condom in your robe?" I squeak.

She shoves the packet into my hand. "Because safety first."

"Oh, honey, I don't think you want to know the answer to that," Margie says from the kitchen.

There's a knock at the door, and before I can put the condom in my purse, Kasen is standing there staring at my hand. He gives me a curious look and I blush.

I'm about to explain, but Aunt Cornelia eyes him up and then me. "Don't take advantage of my niece, Kase, or I'll castrate you myself," she says sharply.

Now it's Kasen who looks rattled. "Of course not, Cornelia."

"Alright then. You two young people have fun...but not

too much fun. I'm in no condition to go bail your asses out of jail," she says as she looks suspiciously between us.

"On that note," I say as I grab my purse, shove the condom in it, and walk out the door with Kasen in tow.

"Have fun!" Margie calls out from the kitchen as Kasen shuts the door.

"Well, that was…uh, interesting," Kasen states as we walk down the stairs.

I groan with embarrassment. "I'm sorry about that. They are, uh…" I trail off because I lack words.

He chuckles. "Oh, I know." He presses his large hand to the small of my back as we exit the building. And something about that feels oddly reassuring.

"So, where to?" I ask as I look up and down the street for a clue as to our destination.

"You said a movie and dinner. So first up is dinner," he announces as he guides me to the right and we begin walking down Hearts Lane.

With the park one building down to the left, it's quiet in this section of the city. No cars can pass through here as the street dead-ends into the park entrance with its wrought iron arch at the start of the walking path. It's a quiet fall evening. Leaves are starting to turn colors on the trees and fall flowers pop with color in window boxes and planters, giving the street the feel of a sleepy suburb instead of a bustling city thoroughfare.

"We're walking there?" I ask.

He shakes his head. "No, my car is parked just here." He motions to a very large, black SUV. If I had imagined the car that most perfectly describes Kasen, this would be it. Not flashy. Large. Practical, although not super practical for city parking. And non-descript.

"No garage?" I ask because I know my aunt keeps her car

in the garage underneath the building. It's not enormous but enough for one car per apartment and then a few guest spots.

"I pulled it around front for you," he says as if the answer is obvious.

He hits the unlock button of his fob and opens the door, holding out his hand to assist me. I accept it and slide into the seat. He waits until I've secured my seat belt before shutting the door and walking around to his side.

He pulls us out onto the street and heads in the direction of the water. I don't ask where we are going but, instead, take in the city as night begins to blanket it in a comfortable darkness broken up by streetlights. I look up as the buildings get taller. We drive through downtown and then a block from the waterfront. He pulls into a small parking lot behind an equally small building.

"Is this the part where you murder me and toss my remains into the water?" I ask.

He leans over the center console, and I can smell his cologne. I take a deep breath. He searches my eyes. I watch the skin around his eyes crinkle as he grins.

"Nah, not tonight," he says and hops out of the car.

I unbuckle my seat belt and he's already opening my door when I go to exit the car. He places his hand on the small of my back again and guides me around the building. I see that it's an Italian restaurant. And it has a beautiful deck next to the walkway along the water. Little fairy lights run in strips criss-crossing the area and space heaters are turned on. There's no one out there and I wonder if they aren't serving outside this evening. It is a little chilly by the water but still unseasonably warm.

We walk inside to the hostess.

"Reservation for Saddler, party of two," he says. I see the young woman do a double take of Kasen before grabbing menus.

"Of course. Right this way," she says as she walks past us and right back out to the patio. I grin.

We follow her outside and she shows us to a table near an outdoor pizza oven along the walkway. We sit and she takes a drink order and then leaves us to peruse the menu.

"Is this OK? Are you too cold?" Kasen asks.

I shake my head. "I was hoping we could eat out here," I admit with a little shrug.

"I may have called in a favor with an acquaintance. A friend's brother is the chef here."

I nod and look down at the menu deciding on my meal. After I make my decision, I gaze out at the water. It's calm, the crests of the little waves glisten with the lights of the walkway.

"You like the water?" he asks, following my gaze.

"Yes," I reply.

"But you said you don't swim well."

I nod. "I'm not a strong swimmer. If you dropped me in the middle of the ocean, I wouldn't last long." I look back out at the water. "I was just remembering snorkeling in Belize a few years ago. Mom took us there. She ran a small race on an island and then we got to go out to the reef for two days. I used a floatation device. It was beautiful." I pause and smile at him. "It reminds me of your tank."

He grins. "Belize has a great reef. I've gone there to dive a few times."

The waitress brings our drinks and takes our order, and we go back to a comfortable silence as we watch a boat go by in the distance.

"I miss having a boat," he admits.

"You had one?" I ask, enjoying the fact that he's sharing something with me.

"I did. But I've been traveling so much that it didn't make

sense to keep it dry docked year-round. So, I sold it last year," he says, his voice tinged with a little sadness.

"Sorry. Maybe you could buy another one," I suggest.

"Maybe, someday."

"So..." I look around. "What should I be practicing?"

"We are practicing. This is just the part where we get to know each other," he explains as he reaches for the bottle of wine he ordered and pours himself some. He offers me his glass and I take a sip. It's surprisingly good for a red wine. I'm more of a white wine drinker.

"It's good," I declare.

He smiles again and takes a sip. Setting down his glass, he pours some for me.

"You said you were staying with your grandmother for a while. Do you speak to her often?" I ask.

I can see a flash of something cross his face. I can't quite tell what he's thinking. Did I overstep? Does he not want to talk about his family? He hasn't said much about them.

"I do," he finally says after a beat.

"So, Scotland, huh?" I ask.

He nods. I wait for him to continue.

"Isle of Barra," he states. "It's a small island in the..."

"Outer Hebrides," I finish.

His eyebrows twitch a little as if he's trying to not react to my knowledge.

"Yes," he says. "My grandfather was a fisherman. Both of my grandparents grew up there. We had to take her to Stornaway to get her treated when I was there. She needed some treatment for her lungs because she had bronchitis and her foot needed X-rays. She couldn't do much around the house after we got back home, so I stayed and helped. I didn't want to leave until I knew she was strong enough to be on her own, aside from when a young woman comes in to help her out during the week."

"I bet it's hard to live out there alone," I say as I remember visiting the islands in middle school with my mom after she had run a race in Scotland.

"It is. So, when did you go there?"

Our food arrives and I spend dinner telling the story of my travels, wondering if I met his grandmother when we spent two nights on the island.

"Where to now?" I ask as we finish eating dessert. Kasen didn't order any but he keeps stealing bites of my gelato.

"Not far," he says.

He pays despite my protest that I should pay, and we walk back to the car.

We drive back toward Hearts Lane and stop at an old theater close to the apartment building. He finds a street spot and we walk a block. It's showing two old movies. I pick one and we get tickets. He asks if I want popcorn and soda and I shake my head. I'm still full from dinner. So we find seats in the theater and settle in to watch the film.

There are only one or two other people in the theater and none near us. I shiver, realizing I'm under an air-conditioning vent.

"Cold?" he asks.

I nod and he leans over, wrapping his arm around my shoulders. I curl up against him as best I can with the armrest blocking me, but he's warm enough that after a few moments, I feel less chilled. The film is a thriller and I think we've both seen it, but we sit and watch in silence. At some point, I feel his thumb making small circles on my upper arm. I don't push away, instead, I snuggle up more against his hard warmth, breathing in his cologne as I watch the ending of the film.

The drive back to one-eleven Hearts Lane doesn't take long. He finds a spot on the street in front of the café and walks me to my aunt's door.

"Did you have fun?" he asks.

"I did. Thank you," I say as I look down at my feet unsure of what to do on this practice date. I steal a glance up at him from beneath my lashes. "Did I do OK?"

He nods. "Yes. When you find a topic to discuss, you are very good at talking to people."

I shrug. "I guess so. I just get nervous."

"Do I make you nervous, little escape artist?" he teases. I want to scream, "Yes!" But instead, I shake my head.

"Good. We should have another practice date, just to make sure you aren't nervous."

"OK. When?" I ask.

"Maybe in a few days? Think about something you'd like to do," he offers. *Kiss you. Maybe make out with you.* Oh my God! I need to stop this. We are only practicing dating. And then I'll be gone in a few weeks. What am I thinking?

"Can I ask you a question?" I say, deciding I might as well take advantage of my dating professor.

"Of course."

"Are you, like, supposed to kiss on the first date?" I ask and I feel the heat creeping up my neck.

His finger comes out and presses my chin up until we're gazing at each other.

"You can. If you're comfortable with that. Not all first dates have to end with a kiss," he explains as if he knows no one has ever told me this.

"Good to know," I state as I search his eyes. "I just..."

"Don't be embarrassed. Just ask me," he encourages.

I lick my lips, and his eyes drop to watch my tongue darting out.

"I need to know if I suck at kissing," I say quickly, the words running together.

"I highly doubt that. Did someone tell you that?" he asks with a frown.

I purse my lips and shake my head. "Not exactly, but it's not like these guys called again, you know?"

"Do you want to practice that?" he inquires, his eyes searching mine.

*Yes!* I take a deep breath because I need to not appear excited about this.

"I think I should."

"OK," he replies slowly.

And without another word, he moves his hand along my jaw and cups it, angling my head a little as he leans down and presses his lips to mine. My eyes are open in surprise, but as he starts to kiss me, my eyelids fall shut. He doesn't force the kiss any deeper, just gently moves his parted lips along mine until I want to crawl up his body. My hands reach out to grip anything to keep me upright. They find his biceps and I grip them firmly as I press myself against him. His tongue gently moves along the seam of my lips. My lips part in surprise and he slowly slides his tongue along mine. He tastes of the wine and gelato we had. It feels right. Like every kiss I had before this one was wrong. His kiss opens a door inside me that I didn't know existed. As he pulls back and looks down at me with hooded eyes and enlarged black pupils, I wonder if he felt it too or if it's just my inexperience speaking.

"Goodnight, Kasen," I manage. "Thank you."

His thumb strokes my cheek gently before dropping away. "You're welcome. And by the way, you get an A-plus," he says, his voice raspy.

"For the date or the kiss?" I ask.

"For both," he answers.

I turn and unlock the door, slipping inside without turning back because I'm afraid I'd literally jump this man for another kiss like that. How am I going to stop myself from falling for my dating teacher?

# CHAPTER THIRTEEN

Kasen

I sit down on my sofa and hold my head in my hands. What the hell was that? I just kissed Piper. I don't mean a practice kiss. That was definitely not a practice kiss. It started out as a practice kiss, but then something in me just snapped. I couldn't get enough of her. God, that took every fiber of my being to pull away. How the hell am I supposed to go out with her again? One pretend date was torture enough. I had to keep reminding myself that the date wasn't real because halfway through that dinner conversation, it felt real as fuck. She knew places around my grandmother's house. No one knows that. It was like she was shining a light into my soul, and my soul had lived in a deep, dark cave for a long time.

I pull out my phone and text the guys' group chat.

Me: I think I want to come to this men's book-club thing.

Gray: You won't regret it.

Drew: Oh? Do tell.

Me: I just think…it'll help me figure out how to help Piper with this dating-lesson thing.

Bray: How many *lessons* are we talking about?

Hutch: Did she fail lesson one?

Me: No. I just told her we could have another practice date. You know, build up her self-confidence.

Drew: Right. Anyhoo, it's tomorrow night. So, go read the book.

A minute later, he emails me a link to a book and I download it. I grab a shower and climb into bed after checking my work email.

The main character is fucking a man on vacation on page five and holy shit. I can't put this book down. I've got to know if the main characters will end up together. I slap my forehead. Of course, they will. God, I'm an idiot. How is Roxy not a millionaire? Because I am most definitely going on a spending spree in her shop tomorrow. This shit is addictive.

———

"He should have done that tongue thing the first time," Hutch says dramatically, waving his hands in the air as if he's discovered a magic world that we all need to see.

"What? No way. He can't give away all his good tricks right away. There has to be a buildup," Bray protests.

"Build up to what? We know they're getting together by halfway through," Gray states.

"No. It's a slow burn," Drew explains with a roll of his eyes.

"Slow burn my ass. They did it on page five," I laugh.

"They didn't know each other. The rest of the book is a slow burn. Page five was a vacation fling," Drew protests.

I start laughing. If someone had said even a day ago that I'd be arguing over a couple in a romance book with my closest friends, I'd have said they had lost their minds. Yet, here I am, arguing about this very topic with my friends. And to top things off, we're sitting in a circle of chairs in the back of Roxy's bookstore, surrounded by countless books with half-naked men on them. She has wine, beer, cheese, and crackers sitting on a small table in the middle of the circle.

"Did you like the overall story?" she asks me.

I look over at her. "No offense, Roxy, but why are you at the guys' book club?"

"Oh, we hold it here once a month. You know, to get a female perspective," Gray explains.

I narrow my eyes as I consider this. Shrugging, I grab a slice of cheese. "So, the woman in the story seems needy. And the guy seems oblivious. Are all romance books like that?" I ask.

Drew starts laughing. "Damn, Kase. Don't beat around the bush." He winks at his innuendo and I groan, but look back to Roxy.

"Nope. Every book in here is different. They all come from a different author's perspective or that author's perspective at a different time. That's what I love about the genre. There's something for everyone," she says with such confidence that I'm silent for a beat.

"I see," I finally say.

"Like, for instance, what is your favorite genre to read?" she asks.

I shrug. I'm not a huge reader nowadays, but I was as I kid. "I guess fantasy," I offer.

She nods and gets up and I watch her walk across the store, grab a book off a shelf, and bring it over to me. She holds it out and I accept it, reading the back cover.

"This is a great romantasy. It's based on Greek mythology. If you like a real classic fantasy story with a prominent romance story, this is a good one to start with. The world-building is fantastic. Consider it a new-customer gift. And let me know what you think," she says as she sits back down next to Gray, who places a hand on her thigh possessively. Damn, when did he become so whipped? He looks like he'd slay a dragon for that woman.

"I will," I reply as I turn the book over to study the cover.

"OK, so what are you guys reading next?" Roxy asks as she takes a sip of wine.

"Billionaires," Drew says.

"We already read one. Dark romance," Gray states.

"When are we reading a medical romance?" Bray asks.

"Football romance," Hutch says.

"We read that last month," Drew whines and Hutch gives him a look which only makes Drew laugh.

There's silence for a minute and the room's attention turns to me.

"Are there any romances where the guy is giving the girl dating lessons?" I ask.

Roxy grins. "There sure are."

Drew sighs. "Fine. But billionaires or why choose better be next month."

Roxy gets back up and walks across the room, coming back with a book. "I suggest this one."

I take it from her and read the back. It might as well be my real life because it certainly sounds like it.

"Perfect," I mutter as Drew rips the book from my hand.

"Oh, is this book three in that series we talked about the other day?" he asks Roxy.

She nods. "But they are interconnected standalones, so you can read them out of order."

"I'll just read the first two as well. You know how I feel about that," he says.

"When's date number two?" Hutch asks.

"Tomorrow night," I say.

"You better get reading, then," he adds, and the others nod in agreement.

Roxy leans forward. "Do you like her?"

I take a sip of beer to give me a moment before I answer. "Of course, I like her. She's beautiful and kind. But I'm not wanting to date. I'm just trying to help her out," I explain.

She raises an eyebrow.

"I'm serious. I'm not boyfriend material," I add.

She looks me up and down. "I don't know, Kasen. I think you might be more boyfriend material than you think you are."

"Hey!" Gray says and Roxy giggles as she sits down in his lap and kisses his cheek.

"Don't worry, I'm already taken," she whispers in his ear, and he squeezes her around the waist, pulling her back against him. A part of me wishes I had that. But then again, that part of me wishes I had a lot of things and people that I don't have.

---

I set the book down. I stayed up late reading it last night. I nearly finished it at lunch today but saved the final chapter for after work. And now, I have the perfect date idea for Piper. I need to get her out of her comfort zone. Date one was a very stereotypical date. I need to make her squirm a bit so she's prepared for anything. I wrack my brain and grin when I figure out what we need to do.

I send Piper a text.

Me: Meet me in the hallway in one hour. Wear comfortable clothes. We will be outdoors.

Piper: Uh, can I get more details?

Me: NO

Piper: Please

Me: I like the politeness, but NO

Piper: You're not making this easy.

Me: Exactly

I get dressed and walk into the hallway. Piper is standing there waiting. She has on black workout pants with a side pocket on the thigh and a fitted zip-up hoodie. It's not her typical clothing and I wonder if this comes from one of the many running events she has been at with her mom. I suddenly realize that just as she doesn't know a lot about me, there are many things I don't know about her...yet.

I hold out my hand and she accepts it. "You ready?"

"Where are we going?" she asks, cocking her head to one side.

"Somewhere," I state as we walk down the stairs.

"Such as?" she asks as I open the door for us. I intentionally parked my car right in front at lunch today, so I unlock it and open the door. She gets in and I close her door and get into the driver's seat.

"You ready?" I ask.

"I guess," she huffs, attempting to be mad, but she's so damn cute, I'm not sure I can take her frustration seriously.

I pat her thigh and she looks over at me. "I promise, it'll be fun. And if not, you can pick what we do for the next practice date."

She smirks. "OK, fair."

And with that, I drive us out of the city.

# CHAPTER FOURTEEN

Piper

It's just starting to get dark. When Kasen turns onto a side road, I look up and see a lit-up sign for a local amusement park and then I see the rides in the distance.

"An amusement park?" I ask, looking around. I haven't been to an amusement park in ages.

"Yep," he replies as he finds us a parking spot.

We get out and he holds out his hand for me. I accept it and we walk up to the ticket booth.

"How's it open still? I thought they closed for the season last month?" I ask as I look around us.

"They open for Halloween events. This is the first one," he explains as he pays for our admissions and we go inside the park. I look around us and realize most people are dressed up in costumes.

Kasen stops at a vendor selling costumes and points to them. "Pick one," he insists.

I look through them and grin when I see matching elf

ears. I point to them and I'm surprised when he grins back at me and asks the kid running the stand for them. He pays and we put them on.

"Do you like roller coasters?" he asks.

"I do, but I also like all those games where you win the giant stuffed animals," I say as I look around us.

"Rides first," he insists and places his hand on my back as he guides me through the maze of pathways to a roller-coaster line. I can't help but notice that Kasen is always on alert. He's constantly scanning the crowds and I wonder as we get in line why he even brought me here.

"Why'd you choose an amusement park?" I ask as he stands behind me, still scanning everyone in our area.

"I read something in a book this week and I thought it'd be a good idea to come to this. It's hard to have practiced conversation in a place like this," he points out as he glances down at me.

"Oh," I reply, not sure what else to say. He's right. This place is filled with distractions and I'm not sure going on this ride is a good idea. I may have a little PTSD from a ride I went on as a kid. We got stuck going up the big hill and it took thirty minutes to get the ride going again. But I decide to be brave. That was years ago and I'm an adult now. I can most definitely handle this.

I tap my foot as we stand there. Suddenly, Kasen's big hand is on my shoulder. I freeze.

"You nervous, little escape artist?" he whispers in my ear and I shiver from the feel of his hot breath on my skin.

"A little," I admit as I steal a glance up at the ride and immediately regret it.

His arm wraps around my front and pulls me back against him. "I got you. Nothing bad will happen," he promises. I want to believe him. But the mind is a crazy place and I swear I feel my blood pressure climbing as we stand there.

I try to focus my attention in front of us, which doesn't help because four teenage boys are standing there having a conversation that I wish I could ignore.

"I bet you puke, bro," one says to a much taller one.

"Fuck off, Jake. I'll be fine. It's Aiden that we have to worry about," he says, hooking his thumb to point at their friend.

"Me? No way. I've ridden this thing like ten times. It's a piece of cake. Except..." He leans in toward them and I feel myself leaning in too. "This one time, a kid threw up and it flew back and hit everyone in the face. It was disgusting."

"Ewww!" the three other boys say in unison.

"Damn, bro, that's gross," the tall one says.

"It was. But my mom bought us T-shirts and the park manager felt bad and gave us one of those lightning passes, so that was cool," the kid says with a shrug.

The quiet kid perks up at that mention. "I got stuck on the one over there last summer." He points to the tallest roller coaster. "We didn't get park passes, but we did have to have one of those fire trucks with the ladders hoist us each down."

"Whoa! That's cool," the short kid says.

I feel myself tremble as I remember getting stuck. Kasen's arm tightens around me and he presses his warm lips to the shell of my ear. "Ignore them. Nothing bad will happen," he assures me.

"What if we get stuck?" I whisper.

"Then, we'll have more time to talk," he offers.

I look up and wince. "What if we get stuck upside down?" I ask, motioning to the one loop in the roller coaster.

He looks up and then tightens his grip on me. He presses his lips to the back of my head and I suddenly am not thinking about the roller coaster. I'm thinking about how badly I want Kasen Saddler to kiss me, again.

The line moves and I realize we are next to get in a car. It's a row of four and we get stuck next to the short and tall kid from in front of us.

The u-shaped harness comes down over us and clicks into place. Kasen reaches over and gives mine a little shake and then does the same to his. I can tell he's satisfied when he drops his hand over mine, which is death-gripping the seat.

"This is supposed to be fun," he says.

"Is now a bad time to tell you that I got stuck on a roller coaster once and I might have PTSD?" I state as I begin to shake a bit.

"Fuck. Seriously?" he asks.

I nod.

"Piper, why didn't you say something?" he asks, and I can tell he feels bad.

"I...it's silly. It was like ten years ago. I should be over that. This is probably a good thing, right?" I squeak as we lunge forward.

"Uh, I'm not a psychologist, but when was the last time you tried to overcome your PTSD?" he inquires.

I don't answer as I look at the giant hill in front of us.

"Piper!" Kasen says loudly.

"Today," I say quietly.

"Fuck. OK, it'll be OK. Maybe, uh, close your eyes," he suggests. I try that but then my other senses take over. I hear the metal clicking as we begin to ascend the first hill. I can hear people around us talking excitedly.

And then, the short kid speaks. "Holy shit! This is so tall! What do you think would happen if we got stuck up here?"

"For the love of...can you guys cool it? My girlfriend here is afraid of heights," Kasen growls.

"Well, riding this is a stupid thing to do, then, isn't it?" the tall kid sneers. But I'm still stuck on the fact that he just called me his girlfriend. Girlfriend? Did he mean that? No.

No, there's no way. He's probably just making that up to get his point across.

"I've killed people for talking less smack than you," Kasen growls.

My eyes fly open and I look over at Kasen in horror. The kid's face is white and he shrinks away from Kasen, muttering something about "crazy adults" to his friend.

"Kasen!" I chastise. "Seriously?"

He looks over at me. "What? The kid was out of line. I don't need some punk-ass little shit making you feel more nervous."

"Be nice! They are just kids," I state as I look over at the boys, but they are both glaring at us. So, I start to look ahead when I realize we are at the precipice and about to go downhill, and fast.

"Oh, shit!" I scream as we fly down the track.

"It's OK!" Kasen yells. But it is definitely not OK. How can this be OK? Why do people like these rides?

"It's not OK! I hate this!" I scream.

"It's almost over!" he yells.

"It is so not almost over!" I retort.

And then it happens. A kid in front of us throws up. This is officially the worst date of my life. Now, I'm covered in vomit, having a panic attack, and I'm two seconds away from peeing my pants out of total fear.

"Shit," Kasen mutters in disgust.

"Gross! Bro, you totally cursed us with that story!" the tall kid screams.

"I'm going to be sick!" the short kid yells and then he vomits on the people behind us.

Twenty seconds later, we pull back into the station and the safety bars pop up. Staff are there ready to clean the ride. I'm thankful it only hit my shoulder and it appears Kasen is also mostly unscathed.

Kasen takes me by the hand and drags me out of the area and into a nearby shop where he promptly purchases us T-shirts and sweatshirts, dumping our dirty ones in a plastic bag. Once we are changed and cleaned up, he buys us sodas and parks us on a bench.

"That was...well, I think I'm over the original PTSD, but I have a whole new one unlocked now," I grumble, breaking the silence.

He groans. "I'm sorry. Fuck. This was supposed to be about getting you out of your comfort zone, not traumatizing you," he mutters.

I start giggling and I can't stop. I keep laughing until I'm doubled over and tears stream down my cheeks. Kasen starts laughing as well.

"Well, I'm definitely out of my comfort zone. Did I pass this test?" I ask as I finally pull myself together.

"With flying colors," he says as he wipes away a tear under his eye.

"Can we, uh, maybe play some games or something? Like, no more rides?" I ask.

He stands and I grip his outstretched hand as he hoists me up and wraps his arms around me, giving me a giant hug. "Thank you for making me laugh. I haven't laughed that hard in a very long time," he murmurs against the top of my head.

"You're welcome. Now, come on, I want a giant stuffed animal," I state as I drag him toward the games.

———

Three hours and two teddy bears and a giant stuffed squid later, we're back at one-eleven Hearts Lane. We're standing at Kasen's apartment door. And I'm anxious for another good-night kiss.

"So," I say as I toe the old carpet in the hallway.

"You want to come in. I can keep these at my place if you like," he says as he holds up an armful of stuffed animals.

I giggle. "That would be great if you don't mind," I say.

Kasen unlocks his door and motions with a teddy bear for me to go inside. I step into his living room and he shuts the door, tossing the stuffed animals onto a nearby chair.

I stand in front of the sofa awkwardly, not sure what I should do.

"Want a drink?" he asks.

"Yes," I say. Liquid courage might help here.

"Have a seat," he says and he goes into his kitchen. I sit down on the edge of the sofa. I vaguely remember one high school date where we ended up back at the guy's house and he kissed me and then tried to grope my boobs, and it was so weird and uncomfortable. He never called again after that night. Maybe I suck at making out.

"What's that look for?" Kasen asks as he comes into the room carrying what looks like two glasses of whiskey.

He hands one to me and I take a sip. It's the good stuff he had the other night. I decide to take it slow this time, so I don't pass out on his couch again.

I set the drink on a coaster on his coffee table and look down at my hands in my lap. "I think...I might suck at making out," I announce.

"I'm sorry, what?" he questions as he sets down his drink.

"I was just remembering a date from high school and I... well, things went really badly. What if I'm OK on the date and then...you know?" I try to explain but I can feel my cheeks heating from my very honest admission.

Kasen's long finger presses under my chin, a touch I'm getting used to, hell, I sort of crave it. I don't normally like people taking control, but for some reason, I'm alright when Kasen does.

"That was high school. We know you can kiss. So, what went wrong?" he asks, searching my eyes.

I let my eyelids fall shut. "I...he...it was just kind of uncomfortable. You know?" I stammer.

"I don't. Use your words, little escape artist. Don't hide," he commands.

I open my eyes and look at him. "He sort of acted like my breasts were dials on an old radio," I attempt to explain as I feel the heat intensify on my face.

"He was a dumb kid. That's not how you turn a woman on, Piper," he states as his hand cups my jaw.

I hold my breath because we are so close that I can see little flecks of green and yellow in his brown eyes.

"How should my date turn me on?" I say, barely audibly because I'm both turned on by just his proximity and also mortified to speak that thought out loud.

"Like this," he says as he leans in and presses slow kisses to my neck, earlobe, jaw, and then finally my lips.

This time, I'm ready for his kiss and I let my lips fall open, welcoming his tongue against mine. The world melts away as I feel Kasen's large hands on my thighs. Shit, I want them higher. I need to alleviate the pressure between my legs or I might go crazy. I squeeze them together, looking for relief.

"Oh, little escape artist. You can't run from your needs. Come here, and I'll show you how it's done. I can most definitely teach you this," he assures me as he pulls me onto his lap, my knees dropping to the sofa on either side of his spread thighs. My core presses to the bulge in his jeans, and God, that feels good.

His hand caresses just under my right breast while the other grips my ass, pressing me more tightly against his erection. How is he as turned on as I am? I don't have time to think again as he starts kissing me, harder and with more need this time. It's like he's searching for the same thing I am. I feel myself grinding against him, but instead of feeling mortified, I feel, empowered.

"That's right. Take what you need, baby," he coos as his lips trail across my jaw. His left hand gently massages my breast and his thumb makes slow circles around my nipple. Fuck, that feels good.

"Good, making out is all about what feels good," he explains, and I realize I just spoke out loud. I feel myself nearing orgasm. I've never done that with a man. One boy tried to feel me beneath my pants once, but his hand got caught in the zipper of my jeans and that ended the date. And just like guy number one, he never called again either.

"Stop thinking, Piper. Just feel." Kasen's voice brings me back to the present as his right hand cups my ass. I feel his hard length press against me as I grind, and fuck, I'm so close. Then suddenly his hand skims the hem of my pants. I freeze.

"We don't have to do anything else if you don't want," he says, not moving a muscle.

"No, it's OK. That's fine. I just..." I trail off because this time, I am embarrassed.

"Just keep rubbing yourself. Let yourself come. You need to learn to let go. This stuff is as much about you feeling good as your partner," he explains as he releases the hem and instead presses his finger against my pants, right over my clit. I gasp at the sensation of feeling someone touch me there.

And just like that, I start grinding again. My eyelids fall closed and I grip his shoulders, riding out a wave that takes its time building and then crashes me onto a shore that I never knew existed. My head slumps into his shoulder and he holds me there.

I'm about to tell him I owe him a hand job or something but my phone starts ringing. I jump off his lap and run to my purse that I dropped by his door. I pull my phone out and see it's Aunt Cornelia.

"Everything OK?" I ask frantically as I answer.

"I sort of got my walker stuck in the bathroom and Margie can't get it loose. Will you be home soon?" she asks.

I sigh. "I'm just coming in now. I'll be there in two seconds," I say as I hang up and turn to Kasen. "I'm sorry. I need to go."

"Go. It's OK. You've had quite enough lessons for one night," he says as he stands, and I can make out the outline in his pants. Holy shit! He's huge.

"OK, goodnight. And uh, thank you," I squeak as I grab my purse and head out of his apartment and into my aunt's, wondering how I'm ever going to top that date, both the good and the bad parts.

# CHAPTER FIFTEEN

Kasen

"Wait. What happened next?" Hutch asks as we run on the treadmills.

"The kid in front of us threw up," I repeat, glancing over at him. He's stopped running, his feet on the outside of the treadmill as he leans over and laughs.

"It was disgusting," I add.

"Oh, I'm not doubting that. I just can't believe that happened. Seriously, how does that happen?" he manages in between laughter.

"Can I finish the story or not?" I growl.

He holds up a hand. "Just...give me a second," he breathes. "OK, OK, please continue." He starts running again and I finish the story of the second date.

"Wow, so you were, like, on your way to third base and then you got cockblocked by an old lady. Man, that's rough," Hutch says when I finish. "Also, that really doesn't seem like a practice date. That seems like a real date."

I groan and stop running, putting my speed down to a cooldown walk. "She said she needed practice. I was *helping* her practice."

Hutch shuts down his treadmill and turns to me. "Be careful, dude. She's young and impressionable and she may see this as more than practice if you keep doing shit like that. You're walking a fine line. *Unless* you do like her."

"What are you, the love doctor? And no, I'm not in the market for a girlfriend," I quip.

"After reading nearly fifty romance books, I feel like one," he says with a shrug as he gets off his treadmill and walks toward the locker room. I stop mine and run after him.

"Fifty?" I confirm, my eyebrows rising.

"What? They are good. I read one almost every night," he explains as we enter the men's room.

"No judgment. If anything, I'm impressed anyone would read that much," I state as I pull off my shirt.

Hutch stands next to me, and I look at him. "For real, man, be careful. Piper is sweet. Don't break her heart."

And with that he heads to the shower and I'm left standing there, wondering if I'm making a huge mistake.

———

Three hours later, I'm still contemplating what I should do about the Piper situation. I push back from my desk, deciding it's time for a mid-morning food break when my phone buzzes. I look down and see it's my grandmother.

"Hello, everything alright?" I ask as I walk toward my kitchen.

"Fine, fine, love. Just thought I'd ring you and see how you were," she answers. Just the sound of her voice is soothing, and I release a breath that I didn't realize I was holding.

"I'm fine," I lie because how could I even explain everything going on in my head?

"Stop lying, Kasen. It's unbecoming," she counters.

Sighing, I pour myself a glass of water and sit down at my counter.

"Out with it," she insists.

My grandmother is the one person that I never lie to. She's my rock. And because of that, I decide to spill it. "I've been thinking a lot about Mum and Dad. Between that and everything that happened before I got discharged and these dating lessons I'm giving my friend, my head is just...in a weird space," I rattle on, meshing so many things together in one long string, it feels like I just knitted a scarf that can be undone by pulling on one end of the yarn.

"Well, well, that's a lot." She pauses and I know she's making herself tea. She always has to have a cup of tea when she talks. I can envision her turning on the kettle and placing her tea bag in her favorite mug with sheep on it.

"I suppose," I reply. I take a sip of water as I listen to her rustling through the box for her tea.

"First, it's a good thing to think about your parents. You never talk about them. And I get it. Their death was tragic and what you experienced when their boat sank was just awful. I still think you should continue with therapy for it, but I can't make you now that you're a grown man." She pauses and I know she's pouring the water in the mug because I just heard the kettle beep. "Second, you should also go to therapy to talk more about that incident that led to you leaving the military. That was another big tragedy. You lost your friend that day. That's a lot of loss, Kasen. Especially when you were so young." She pauses once more, and this time, she's most definitely sipping her tea. "Now tell me about this friend."

I smile as I listen to her footsteps on her wooden floor. I

can tell she's still walking slower after her injury. But the fact that she is up and around makes me feel a little better. There's a pause and I know she's reached her chair by the window. The one that overlooks the water. I wonder if it's raining there today or if the sun is reflecting off the waves.

"Her name is Piper. She just graduated college. She's Cornelia's niece and is staying there to help her after her ankle surgery. We've hung out a few times. She's not had much dating experience and I offered to take her on a few practice dates," I start. She doesn't say anything, so I continue. "We've gone out on two dates and...I think I may have more feelings for her than I thought I did."

"That's wonderful news. Just ask her out on a proper date, then," she encourages.

"We both know that I'm too messed up for a relationship. She deserves better than that," I say as I swirl the water in my glass.

"Kasen Ian Saddler! That is not true! You are the kindest, most generous, and loving grandson in the world. Any woman would be lucky to call you her boyfriend. And you deserve love, my dear boy. Do not deprive yourself of the love you deserve," she says and I want to believe her. But I'm not sure I can.

I grunt a "right."

"I'm serious. And what's the harm in going to a therapist? You could at least try that. Go once, if it's so awful, then at least you can say you tried it," she says. She's told me this so many times. And she's not wrong. I've been thinking about it lately. When she got sick and injured herself and needed my help, it made me realize how petrified I was of losing her. Besides my friends, she's all I have left. She spent those nearly twelve weeks encouraging me to go to the little café in town where the Wi-Fi was better and I could get cell reception. She wanted me to talk with my friends, but all I cared about was making sure she was fine. I can't imagine my life without her and I hate that I'm so far away. I thought several times about moving back to the island, but my work requires me to travel and have internet connections that aren't possible there and she refuses to leave. We reached an impasse eventually and she told me to, and I quote, "Get your arse back home and live your own damn life. I got it from here."

"Maybe I will," I say. She made me go to therapy after my parents died and I had to go for a few months after the incident on the beach during my last military mission. But after getting discharged, I started skipping out on the therapy and eventually just stopped going altogether. It was easier to push all the bad memories into a box in the way back of my brain and store it in some unused closet there, where I never thought about it because thinking about those tragedies makes them too real.

"Good. Alright then, my job is done for today. I'm going to meet Gwen at the pub later. Go call her. You haven't said much about her, but I can tell she's special just by the tone of your voice," she states.

"She is," I mumble, having a hard time saying it out loud.

"Very well then, I'll look forward to meeting her someday. Have a good day," she says.

"Bye," I reply as I hang up and text Bray before I lose the nerve to ask him this.

Me: Hey, know any good therapists?

Bray: About damn time.

Me: What the hell?

Bray: Randy Philips. Here's his contact info.

I save the contact info and call, making an appointment for the following week. One time. I'll try it one time. What's the worst that can happen? I grimace because I already know the worst things that can happen. And as if the world wants to prove that my entire life isn't shit, Piper texts me.

Piper: Do you think she could have lost the necklace at the pool? She said something about aquatic aerobics the day before the accident.

I try to remember. Cornelia and Margie both take a class at the pool. It's possible she lost it there.

Me: It's possible. Shall we go for a swim?

Piper: I think we should. I mean, I'll try to swim and you can swim laps around me.

Me: (laughing emoji) I'm free tonight.

Piper: Sounds like we're working out this evening.

Just the mere idea of spending the evening with her puts me in a good mood. She's like a ray of sunshine in my otherwise stormy world.

# CHAPTER SIXTEEN

Piper

I pull the strap on my bikini. Damn it! I should have packed a one-piece. Kasen and I are at the gym about to join a water aerobics class. We are easily the youngest people here by a good three decades. And yet, I'm still feeling very self-conscious about what I have on.

I tighten the robe around me and walk to the edge of the pool. I dip my toe in the water and am relieved to find that it's not freezing. Phew!

Three ladies who look about eighty years old are in the pool with the instructor and a few more women who are maybe in their sixties are in the back of the pool. I toss my robe on a chair and climb into the shallow end.

A moment later, Kasen walks in, and all seven women turn to stare at him.

It takes five or so seconds for me to realize I'm holding my breath. Kasen has on swim trunks, but he looks like a Ken doll.

"Hello, ladies, mind if I join you?" he asks.

He's met by a chorus of "yes" and "of course" and "come on in" and "there's room next to me." He dives in and swims over near me.

"Hi," I say as I attempt to tread water. But I probably look like a wet dog that hasn't yet discovered it can swim.

"Hello," he replies.

We don't have much time for anything else as the instructor begins the class. We start in the shallow end with some water weights and then we do some deeper water exercises and then end back in the shallow part. I get a special pool noodle to help me in the deep end after the instructor says that no one is dying on her watch.

Aside from the embarrassment of my lack of swimming abilities, it's a surprisingly good workout. My core muscles are feeling it by the end of the class. Kasen and I have also been trying to check around the pool for the necklace, but so far we haven't seen it.

"OK, last stretch. Raise those arms high. Very good," the instructor, whose name is Brittany, says to us. I keep stretching enjoying the feeling when all of a sudden, I feel a pop.

I look down and immediately cover my chest. Holy shit! My left bikini strap just snapped.

"Everything OK?" Kasen asks as he swims over to me.

"I...uh...can you grab my robe for me?" I ask.

"What's wrong, honey?" an older lady named Linda asks.

"Oh, I...am having a wardrobe malfunction," I whisper as I use one hand to motion to my bikini strap that my other hand is holding up.

"Oops. That's no good. Clarice, Piper here needs some help with her top. Remember when Kathleen popped her bathing suit strap. Same problem," she calls out.

I feel my face darken with embarrassment as I am suddenly surrounded by a flock of older women.

"I have a bobby pin in my bag," one says.

"We could tie it behind your head," another offers.

"No, look, it won't work," her friend says.

"Ladies, I have her robe here," Kasen states as he holds out my robe. Everyone looks up at him because he's dripping wet and the outline of his dick is...apparent.

"Are you two dating?" Linda asks me.

I have no idea how to answer that. Yes. No. Define dating. So I just go with it. "Not really."

"Well, you should because men that look like that do not come around very often," she says.

"OK, ladies, we need to form a protective circle," Linda declares, and I find myself surrounded by all seven women as I get out of the pool. They part like water going around a sandbar as Kasen enters the circle and wraps me in my robe.

"All better," he whispers as he ties the sash, his hands lingering there for a moment as our gazes stay fixed on each other.

"You decent now?" a woman asks me.

"Yes. I am. Thank you all so much," I say to my new gym friends.

"Did you find that necklace you were looking for?" Linda asks. At some point during class, Kasen had to explain our weird behavior. That led to a two-minute class break and everyone floating around to look, but even then we didn't find it.

"No," I say. "I guess she must have left it somewhere else. But if anyone finds it, please let me know."

"We will," Linda says.

And with that, I scurry into the women's locker room to change.

When I come out, Kasen is standing by the front desk

talking to a young woman who might as well have those googly heart eyes that cartoon characters get. Kasen seems somewhat unaffected by her. But when his gaze meets mine, it's as if the other woman no longer exists. He doesn't even say goodbye, he just walks straight over to me.

"You OK?" he asks as he pushes a lock of hair away from my face. It's such an intimate touch, yet I don't shy away from it. In fact, I sort of like that he did that.

"Yes," I reply.

"Good. Because I had another idea about where we could look. But...uh, you might need another bathing suit," he says.

"Oh. I don't have one," I state. "I only brought the one."

"We sell them here," the woman he was speaking to says as if she's been part of our conversation the entire time.

"How much?" Kasen asks.

"Eighty dollars," she replies as she pulls out my size.

He reaches into his pocket, pulls out a card, and taps it against the scanner.

"OK, let's go back to the apartment and you can change," he says.

I'm confused, but I follow him the two blocks back. He doesn't say where we are going, and for some reason, I don't ask. I'm too fixated on his warm hand that is covering mine. His thumb strokes the back of my hand as we walk in silence, our gym bags swinging over our shoulders. I find myself pressing against him as we walk. He keeps me on the inside of the sidewalk. I notice again how he's scanning his surroundings. Kasen always seems to be on high alert. Does the man ever stop paying attention to everything around him?

When we get back to his apartment, I turn to my aunt's door. "Let me get her settled," I say as I motion to the door.

"OK. Put on that bathing suit and meet me on the roof," he says.

I nod and hurry inside, shutting the door behind me and leaning against it.

"How was the class?" Aunt Cornelia asks.

"It was fun. No necklace though," I say. "Bathroom?"

She nods and I help her get up and to the bathroom. "I think Kasen has a sweet spot for you," she declares as I bring her back to the chair and she settles into it.

"Nah. But he is a good friend," I correct, but inside I'm warring with myself. Could he like me? No, there's no possible way. "Speaking of that. He wants to go look for the necklace on the roof. So, I'll be upstairs if you need me."

"OK," she says as she sips her water and starts knitting.

I change quickly and put a long T-shirt over my bathing suit. It's a warm fall day, but the roof is likely to be cold. I bring a towel and head upstairs.

When I get to the roof, I look over and see Kasen is back in his swim trunks and sitting on the edge of a hot tub.

"I forgot about the hot tub," I say as I walk over to him and pull my shirt off. I join him on the edge, our feet dangling into the bubbling hot water, which feels amazing. It's a little chilly up here but not with the hot tub going.

"Cornelia was up here before the fall. So I thought, maybe we could check the greenhouse and water the plants and check the hot tub," he explains.

"I need to finish painting some of those pots," I state as I point to the greenhouse.

"We'll have time later," he says, his eyes dipping to my rising chest. "Get in before you get cold."

I slide into the water and he joins me. I swallow as I watch him put his giant arms across the edge of the hot tub. I decide to sit in the crook of his arm. Our hips touch as I dangle my feet in the water.

"I don't see it in here," I state as I look around in between the bubbles.

"No, me either," he says but he's not looking in the water, he's looking at me. My gaze drops to his lips where a single drop of water sits, probably from the bubbling hot tub. I'm not sure what happens next, but I somehow end up in his lap. Leaning forward, I lick the drop of water from his bottom lip.

"Fuck, little escape artist. That was hot," he murmurs against my lips.

"You had water," I explain as if that was a good reason to lick his lip.

"I have water in a lot of places," he teases and I groan when he thrusts his hips against my core.

"Do it again," he commands. I frown in confusion, but he leans his head toward mine and I know he means that I should lick his lip again.

My tongue darts out and this time his lips open and his tongue slides along mine. My arms reach around his neck and pull him closer to me. His hands grip my waist, pressing me down into him.

I start grinding against him as we kiss. Is this what sex is like? Because if it's half as good as this, then I have clearly been missing out for a long time.

"Kasen," I whisper as I pull back.

"What is it, baby?" he coos as he continues to press a few gentle kisses to my jaw. "Is..." I trail off because I realize how embarrassing of a question it is.

He cups my face and we stare at each other.

"What?" His eyes search mine.

"Sex," I whisper.

His brows furrow.

"What's it...like?" I clarify.

His lips form a small smile. "Oh, baby, it's good, so good. Better than anything you can imagine. And if you have the right partner, even better," he tries to explain.

"How do you know if you have the right partner?" I feel my cheeks heat. Why am I asking him these questions? I should be more embarrassed but I feel like I can trust him. My parents never really spoke about sex and my grandmother and great-aunt are too mortifying in their responses for such a discussion and I have no siblings and no friends close enough that I would trust to discuss the topic. So, I guess that leaves Kasen and he has agreed to teach me. I suppose it makes sense to ask him.

His hand cups my jaw. "You'll feel it," he replies and kisses me again.

"Mom, I know I left him..." We hear Ava's voice and I push away from Kasen like he has some highly contagious disease.

"Whatcha doin'?" Ava says with a smirk. This kid is observant for being so young.

"Playing mermaids. What are you doing?" I ask her.

She frowns because she clearly did not expect my answer.

"Looking for...Mr. Pickles!" she screams in delight as she runs past us to a lounge chair and pulls out a giant stuffed donkey.

"Found him, Mom!" she says as Carly steps out onto the roof.

"Oh, hey," she says when she sees us. "Pardon us. We'll be going." She grabs Ava and heads to the door.

"Uh, do you think we should have explained the pretend dating thing?" I ask, making a mental note to talk with her later.

He waves his hand. "No, but you're breaking out in a rash. We should probably get out of here," he says. I look down to find my chest is splotchy red. Frowning, I realize I can smell a chemical other than chlorine.

"What does Al clean the hot tub with?" I ask.

"Some special pool chemical, why?" Kasen asks as he gets

out of the hot tub and holds out his hand. I take it and curse under my breath.

"I think I'm allergic to it," I groan.

"Come on, let's go get you some medicine," he says as he leads me back downstairs. I know this isn't a third pretend date, but it's starting to feel like it. All of this is starting to feel very not pretend and I sort of like that. But does Kasen?

# CHAPTER SEVENTEEN

Kasen

I knock on Cornelia and Margie's door the next afternoon. I'd texted Piper in the morning and she claimed she was fine, but I need to see it for myself. Margie opens the door.

"Well, hello there. Kasen's here!" she calls out as she ushers me inside. I walk into the living room, where I find Cornelia sitting up with one boot-clad foot and leg propped on an ottoman.

I frown. "Is the chair not working?" I walk over to examine the footrest of the chair.

She waves me away. "It's fine. I just wanted my good leg to feel normal for a few minutes. Next week, I'm allowed to start putting a little weight on it," she says with a big grin.

"That's good news," I reply as I look around for Piper but don't see her. She had quite a few hives after the hot tub last night and insisted she just needed some allergy meds and a good night's sleep. I had given her some allergy medicine but then she had said she didn't want to bother me if she needed more, and before I could protest, she left.

"She's resting in my room," Cornelia says. "Quite the allergic reaction she had. Good thing you gave her that allergy medicine right away. I fortunately still had some cream for her to put on it."

I don't move, unsure of what to do. If I run down the hall, will I look desperate? This is all supposed to be for practice, not for real.

"Why don't you go check on her?" Margie suggests. "I'm filling in with our patient out here."

She motions to Cornelia, who rolls her eyes. "I'm fine. This ankle has so much metal in it, it might as well be made of titanium."

I give them a nod and head down the hall, stopping at Cornelia's door. I knock, but there's no answer. I crack open the door and find a very passed-out Piper. I walk into the room and sit on the edge of the bed. Her hair is fanned out over the pillow. Her skin looks better but she still has a few hives on her chest and arms. I feel awful. It's my fault she's hurting. I start to stand but her hand flies out and grabs my arm.

"Kasen, don't go," she whispers as she opens her eyes.

I kick off my shoes and crawl onto the bed, pulling her against me gently. I kiss the top of her head as she snuggles into my chest. "You OK, little escape artist?" I ask.

"I'm better now," she sighs as her body relaxes. I stroke her hair.

"When did you last take medicine?" I ask.

"An hour ago," she murmurs, her voice barely audible.

"Go to sleep," I urge because she clearly needs a nap.

I sit there in silence as I watch her fall back asleep, wondering what I should do next. I haven't wanted more with a woman in a long time. But right now, holding her, I feel free from all my nightmares. Every past trauma has melted away. I'm calm and I'm never calm. It's only been a few weeks since I met her, and I can already feel the ways she's changing me.

I hold her tighter, afraid if I don't, she'll disappear. Eventually, her soft breaths lull me to sleep too.

———

"Wake up, sleeping beauties. It's happy hour time," Margie's voice calls out from the door.

I open my eyes and realize I fell asleep. Piper stirs in my arms. I look down and see her welts are lessening. I only see one or two left. Her face is completely back to normal.

"How do you feel?" I ask.

She's quiet for a beat as she assesses herself. "Better," she finally says as she sits up and looks around.

"I...I'm sorry," she whispers.

"For what?"

"I fell asleep on you," she says quietly.

I chuckle. "I fell asleep too."

She smiles. "Shall we go up for drinks?"

I brush some hair away from her eye and tuck it behind her ear. Fuck. The way she looks at me makes me feel things I shouldn't. An entire life that I know I can't have flashes before my eyes. Waking up with Piper every morning. A house full of kids. Christmas at my grandmother's house. I wipe away my thoughts as I rub my eyes. That's a future that won't exist. Not now, not ever.

"What?" Piper asks, cocking her head a little to one side. Her lips are puffy from sleep and her cheeks rosy. The urge to kiss her overwhelms me.

I lean in and place a soft kiss on those lips. Her eyes fall closed.

"Is this what it should be like with a real boyfriend?" she asks against my lips. "Am I...doing this right?"

"You're a natural, little escape artist. Now, come on, let's go," I say as I place another light peck on her lips and then crawl out of bed.

"You two were out like babies. I didn't have the heart to wake you," Margie says as we emerge from the bedroom.

"Guess I was more tired than I thought," I say as I rub the back of my head.

"You look better, dear," Cornelia says to Piper. I look over and notice her last two hives are nearly gone.

"Yeah, I feel better. We're going up to happy hour. You want us to bring you anything?" Piper asks her aunt.

"Nah. I could use a nap myself," she says with a yawn.

Margie collects bowls of soup the two of them clearly have been eating and takes them to the kitchen.

"You hungry?" I ask Piper. She shakes her head. I pull out my phone and text Cam.

Me: Can you bring over some pastries for happy hour?

Cam: Yep. Can do. I'll send them over with Drew. I'm working late tonight.

Me: Thanks.

"Come on," I say to Piper. I look back in the kitchen. "Margie, you coming?"

"I'll be up in a few," she calls out.

We walk upstairs and find Hutch and Bray at their usual seats at the bar. Al's serving them. Carly is talking to Bray and Ava is coloring at the table near the bar.

She pops her head up and smiles at me. "I'm drawing you," she says with a smile.

"Oh?" I mutter, half paying attention as I motion to Al for a drink.

"Let's see," Piper says cheerfully as she walks over to her. Ava holds up her drawing.

It's a pool or a tub or something and two people.

*Oh, God. Is that...did she draw Piper and me in the hot tub?*

Piper looks back at me, her eyes wide.

"That's very nice. You want me to draw you," Piper says, seemingly pulling herself together so as not to draw attention to what Ava likely saw in the hot tub. Crap. Have I taken this pretend dating instructor thing too far? Probably. Do I want to take it further? Yes.

Fuck. I'm so screwed.

"Sure," Ava says excitedly. She hands Piper some paper and slides her giant crayon and colored pencil set across the table.

"Piper, you want a drink?" Al asks.

"Just some club soda for me, tonight," she says as she begins drawing.

He pours her some while Hutch tells about his latest attempt at trying to catch the Guardian of Hearts Lane Park.

"I was thinking about getting a drone," he says.

"It's heavily wooded back there. You won't see anything," I point out as Al hands me Piper's drink. I turn to give it to her and stop as I set it down. Her drawing of Ava is...amazing.

"Wow," I manage.

She holds up the drawing next to Ava. "Not bad," she says with a smile.

"Let me see," Ava says as she grabs the paper. "It looks just like me!" she squeals and shows Carly.

"You're really good," Carly agrees.

"Thanks," Piper responds.

"I think you should draw all of us," Hutch says as he looks at the sketch and then looks down at Ava's drawing. "What did you draw, Ava?"

Oh fuck.

"Mr. Kasen and Miss Piper," she says without looking up from her next drawing.

"Oh? Here?" Hutch asks.

"Yeah, over there," Ava says, keeping her head down as she draws, but raising a single finger to point to the hot tub.

"Huh, interesting," Hutch states as he looks from me to Piper. I give him a pointed look and he smirks.

I flip him off and go back to watching Piper.

"You should do that professionally," Carly interjects as she leans over the table.

"I'd love to, someday," Piper says as she finishes a sketch of Al serving Hutch and Bray. "I've always wanted to illustrate kids' books."

"I can see that. You have an eye for detail," Carly says.

"I guess so. My mom always says that I was an observant child, that I saw things most adults overlook," Piper says as she continues to draw without looking up at anyone.

I glance down and see she's drawing me. But unlike the other drawings where she kept looking up at the people, she doesn't look at me. She's drawing me completely from memory as if she's memorized every line of my body. Has she been watching me as much as I've been watching her?

"There," she says as she finishes, pushing the paper toward me. I look...good. Even the scar above my eye looks... well, like a distinguished mark of a gentleman. Is this how she sees me? My gaze finds hers. "It's how I see you," she confirms quietly for my ears only.

And for the first time in a long time...I feel seen.

# CHAPTER EIGHTEEN

Piper

"You're so talented," Kasen says as he looks at the portrait I drew of him. It's on his fridge with a single magnet that he stole from Margie's collection. He said he wanted to keep my drawing and I told him it was fridge art. He walked into my aunt's kitchen and grabbed a magnet that says, "I like to cook with wine. Sometimes I even put it in the food." Then he grabbed my hand and marched us back to his place, where he unceremoniously stuck my picture on his fridge.

Now, I'm sitting here as we brainstorm for any other places we could look for my aunt's necklace. She's basically given up hope that we can find it. And I'm not far behind.

Today, my aunt graduated to being able to walk on her own. She's asked me to stay for another week or two and I've agreed. The man standing in front of me is a big reason that I don't want to leave. I love our daily talks. I love everything about him. But I know there's more to him than what he's shared. He's a mystery that I need to solve. I'm not sure I can leave until I do.

"Thanks," I murmur as I watch Kasen make our drinks. It's become a bit of a routine. Our own private happy hour. He claims this will help me with dating and conversation with men, but mostly we discuss a show we're both watching or he tells me funny stories about his teenage years in Scotland. He still hasn't told me much about his parents or his time in the military, but I feel like we're getting closer to him sharing more. He's this big, burly man, but I think he's not so strong on the inside.

"Have you ever offered your artistic services to authors?" he asks, sliding my drink across the counter to me.

I swirl the amber liquid in my glass. "No," I say quietly. I don't elaborate. Would I love drawing for books? Yes. Would I love to paint for galleries? Yes. Heck, I would do any job that involved my artistic talents, but those jobs are hard to find.

Kasen walks around the counter and sits down next to me. "What do you want in life?"

I feel my eyes widen and eyebrows rise involuntarily as I react to his big question. "That's...uh...gosh, I don't know," I stumble over my words as I rack my brain for an answer.

He sets his glass down and takes my hands in his, our gazes locking. "Think about one year from now. Just a single year. If you could choose what you'd be doing, what would it be?" he asks, his eyes searching mine. He's so sincere.

*I'd want to be here with you.* God, I'm an idiot. It's probably for the best that I'm leaving in another week or two. My father reached out last week and offered up his guesthouse for me to stay in for a while. I've seriously been contemplating going out to Seattle to stay with him. I could clear my head of these delusional cobwebs I have about a future with

Kasen where I illustrate books and sit in the park drawing frogs on lily pads.

"Well?" he prods.

"I, uh, maybe illustrating books or making book art?" I reply, but it comes out more of a question than a statement.

He's still for a few seconds and then hops off his stool.

"Come on, we're going to see Roxy," he announces as he holds out his hand to me, a motion I've become all too familiar with, a motion that brings me immense comfort. After a lifetime of wanting that from my parents, it's like he senses I need it even when I don't realize that myself.

"OK," I say in a voice that sounds completely unsure.

We walk downstairs, hand in hand. He ushers me into the bookstore and waves to Roxy who's sitting behind the desk, her feet are up on a nearby chair. She's reading a book.

"Hey, you looking for a new read?" she asks him as she sets her book down.

I look at Kasen with a raised eyebrow.

"No, we're here about Piper," he says, quickly deflecting attention onto me. But my curiosity is piqued. I need to know what he's been reading.

"Yeah, any good books you can recommend Kasen here? Or me?" I ask innocently.

Kasen narrows his eyes, and I smirk.

"Of course, let's find you both something," she says excitedly as she gets up and walks toward a shelf.

"Jocelyn? Did the new inventory get shelved yet?" she calls out as she surveys the shelf.

"Yep, it's all out there," Jocelyn's disembodied voice says from behind another shelf.

"Actually," Kasen starts and Roxy stops to look at him. "We were curious if you know any authors who would want to hire Piper to do...what did you call it the other day?" He pauses and then snaps his fingers. "Character art."

Her eyes look from me to Kasen. Roxy and Jocelyn had come up near the end of happy hour when I was drawing people. I follow her gaze as she looks behind her desk and I see my drawing of her sitting out with some other book-related things.

"Well, funny you should mention that. The other day, an author friend of mine popped in to chat about an upcoming release she's having and she saw your drawing and really liked it. I've been meaning to ask you if you did character art, but I keep forgetting to text you. So, do you?" she asks.

"Like, what exactly do you mean?" I question.

Roxy walks over to a table and picks up a few items. "This," she says as she points to a cover. "And this." She holds up a postcard with an illustrated couple. "And also this," she says as she picks up a magnet and a sticker with illustrated characters.

I walk over to her and examine each item. Can I do this? Yes. She hands me some more postcards. Yeah, I could do that.

"Yes. I can draw things like this," I say as I flip through a stack of illustrated character art.

"Really?" she asks, her voice rising an octave.

"Yeah. I'd just need character descriptions," I explain as I place the cards back down into a basket on a table.

"Then, I have some clients for you. I'll send out an email, but first, do you have a portfolio or a website?" she asks.

I shudder. I do have a website, but it's super out of date and also is more focused on the graphic design stuff I did in college since I thought that would be the easiest career to obtain once I graduated.

"Give me a week to pull my art together," I say.

"Wonderful, let me know when it's ready and I'll share it with my author newsletter," she offers.

"Seriously?" I ask.

She nods and smiles. "Yes, absolutely. You are very talented."

Since Aunt Cornelia needs my help less and less each day, it's the perfect time to spend a few afternoons drawing. I could easily switch my website around in a week. For the first time in a long time, I feel excited.

"Thanks!" I say as I pull Roxy in for a hug.

"Anytime," she replies. She looks down at her watch. "Anyone want a coffee?"

Kasen laughs. "Roxy, it's like half past five. Do you even sleep?"

The bell on the door rings and we all look over to see Gray come into the store. "She doesn't sleep much," he says with a smirk.

Roxy rolls her eyes. "Yes, I sleep. I just don't have coffee right before bed."

"That'll change," Kasen mumbles as Gray walks up to Roxy and kisses her. I practically swoon. Is that how couples act when they are in love? Kissing like they don't care if anyone else sees them. For the briefest of moments, I wish I could experience that type of connection. Maybe, someday.

"I should really get back to Aunt Cornelia. Margie wants to make dough for bagels. And needs help, since my aunt isn't quite up to the task yet," I explain.

"OK, well, see you guys later," Roxy says from over Gray's shoulder.

We leave as Gray goes in for another kiss.

"You didn't finish your whiskey yet," Kasen says as we opt to take the sketchy elevator.

"Right. I can only stay a few more minutes though. I did promise Margie I'd help tonight," I explain.

"Does this mean tomorrow she'll have fresh bagels for breakfast?" he asks as we exit the elevator and he unlocks his door.

"Yep. If all goes as planned," I say as I sit back down and grab my drink.

"So, we're going to make you a famous illustrator, huh?" he says with a big smile that has me setting my drink back down and pulling him into a hug.

"Thank you, Kasen," I whisper in his ear as I squeeze around his neck more tightly, burying my face in his neck and inhaling his woodsy cologne.

He doesn't move at first, but then slowly he wraps his arms around me and pulls me off my chair and onto his lap. We sit there for a long time, just hugging. Not even in a sexual way, just being there, together.

"Finish your drink, love," he murmurs as he places a platonic kiss on the top of my head. He sets me on my stool and we clink glasses and each sip our whiskey.

It doesn't take long for me to finish as I tell him my ideas for character art. He's quiet and listens to me. I want to say, I want to make sexy character art, inspired by you, but I don't have the bravery to speak the words out loud. I still have no idea what I'm doing in the bedroom.

As Kasen shows me out, a needy feeling begins building inside of me. What if I asked Kasen to help me lose my virginity? I trust him. From the way he kisses and touches me, I'd bet he'd be good at sex. He knows way more than I do. And then I'd know what all the fuss is about. I wouldn't have to pretend to know when women talk about it at parties. I wouldn't be embarrassed to admit I hadn't done it yet. I know I shouldn't be embarrassed, but I sort of am. It's like men are aliens and I've never had an encounter.

"What?" Kasen asks as I turn to go back to my aunt's.

"Nothing, just, uh, thinking more about the pretend dating thing," I say because it's not a total lie.

"Oh? Maybe we should have another pretend date?" he suggests.

"I think that's a great idea," I agree, attempting to rein in my excitement.

"OK, I'll figure out a plan for this coming weekend," he offers as he watches me unlock the door.

"Sounds good. Goodnight, Kasen," I say.

"Goodnight, illustrator," he replies, and I smile as I turn, loving my new nickname.

# CHAPTER NINETEEN

Kasen

I couldn't sleep last night, so I got up and scoured the building for Cornelia's necklace. Spoiler alert: I didn't find it.

Now, I'm downing coffee at the café.

"Dude, that's your fourth coffee in as many hours. I never like to turn down customers but maybe try to drink some water," Cam says as she pushes a bottle of water toward me.

"I need to get back to work. I'm just exhausted," I admit.

I'm also nervous. I have my first appointment this afternoon with the therapist that Bray recommended. I hate therapy. It's never worked and I feel stupid trying again, but something deep down keeps gnawing at me that I need to work on myself.

"Water," she states again and pushes it closer to me.

I glare at her, and she crosses her arms. I sigh, take the water, and head back to my apartment. I wrap up where I was with my project and get on the telehealth call.

A man appears on the screen after a few seconds.

"Kasen Saddler?" he asks. He's about my age and is clean-shaven, wearing glasses, and in the background, I see a photo of men in Navy uniforms. Fucking Bray. He knew that'd make it easier for me.

"Yeah," I answer and we begin our session.

————

One hour later, I need some air. I walk up to the roof and find Piper sitting in the greenhouse painting a pot. I stand by the door for a long time. I watch the way her hair moves with her head. The way she scrunches her nose and sticks out her tongue as she concentrates. The way she smiles when she gets it how she wants it. She's not putting on an act for anyone. She's just being authentically herself.

Finally, her head moves and her gaze meets mine. I grin as I see a swatch of paint on her right cheek. She's a wonderful, beautiful mess. She's perfection. All the heavy thoughts from the past hour melt away like ice on a hot summer day. I'm not thinking of the device buried in the sand on the beach where it killed my friend Tyler. I'm not thinking of the boat sinking and my parents disappearing into the dark, stormy night. No, I'm just thinking about Piper, and how she's like a sun so bright she blinds me from seeing all those dark things.

She sets down her paintbrush and wipes her hands on an old rag. Slowly, she walks over to me. I can see her brows furrow as she approaches me, and then without explanation, she wraps her arms around my midsection and pulls me against her. Her cheek presses against my chest and I bring my arms up and around her shoulders. I press my lips to the top of her head and inhale. I can smell her floral shampoo. It's a smell that's becoming so familiar. I don't know what type it is, but that smell will forever remind me of Piper.

"Are you OK?" she asks, not moving.

"I am now," I reply because it's the truth. "And here I thought you'd be excited to have me out of your hair."

"What do you mean?" I ask, pulling back a bit so I can look her in the face.

"Aunt Cornelia has her big checkup in another week and a half and then I'm going to stay with my dad for a while," she explains.

"Your dad?"

"Yeah. He offered up his guesthouse out in Seattle. So, I figured I'd try out life out there. I need to eventually figure out where I'm supposed to be," she says with a shrug.

*With me. That's where you're supposed to be.*

"Oh?" I manage.

She pushes away from me, and I nearly reach out to pull her back. But I just stand there watching her.

"Why does adulting have to be so...so complicated?" she asks.

"Because it's a choose-your-own-adventure except you can't control what's happening, like *Jumanji*," I say, feeling quite a bit of the last part.

She steps back to me, searching my eyes. "Will you tell me what happened to you? Someday?"

I swallow. I want to tell her everything, but I'm also afraid to say a word. What if she runs away? What if she sees how broken I am and decides it's too bad? I've liked this putting-me-on-a-pedestal thing. I like the way she looks at me as if I know everything and can protect her from all of it. It makes me feel powerful again, even if just for a moment.

"You don't want to hear those stories, illustrator," I whisper as I cup her cheek. She leans her head against my hand.

"Maybe I do," she says in a low murmur. She turns her head a little and places a soft kiss on my palm. Fuck, she's so innocent, yet it's like she knows just how to touch me.

"You should get back to your painting," I state as I motion toward the pot. She grabs my hand and tugs me toward the greenhouse. She pats a stool and I sit.

"Tell me about your worst day," she says as she turns and starts to paint.

Something about her not facing me gives me the courage to tell her something, just one thing. I can do that much, for her.

"I can tell you about my first worst day," I start.

She nods but doesn't speak. So I continue.

"I lived with my parents in Maine. My dad was a fisherman and my mom sometimes went out on the boat with him when his two crew were unavailable. I had just turned fourteen." I pause as I remember that day. I had been so excited to get to go fishing and help. I wouldn't have admitted that to my parents, but it was the truth.

"My dad had me and my mom helping, since Mo and Butch weren't available. We left later than he had wanted to. There was a storm coming and he wanted to get in before it hit. But the storm rolled in faster than he expected. Lightning hit our motor. A giant wave rolled the boat. And in the storm and confusion, I got separated from them. I managed to grab on to a dinghy and I clung to it for two hours before the Coast Guard found me. They never recovered my parents' bodies," I say as I close my eyes, willing the memories to subside.

I feel two small, soft hands on mine and I open my eyes.

"I'm sorry that happened to you," she says as we stare at each other.

"It was a long time ago," I state because it was.

"Yes, but that doesn't make a difference. My parents were divorced a long time ago, and I still remember their fights. That stuff doesn't go away. And when you remember it, it's like it happened yesterday. Like an old wound that never healed right and sometimes just pops open," she says and the sadness in her voice breaks my heart. She steps between my legs. I pull her against me, and she holds me tightly. I feel like we're each other's life vests in a stormy ocean. How will I ever be able to let her go?

"Kasen," she says.

"What, baby?" I say quietly.

"I sort of need to tell you something," she says and I lean back and look at her. She looks nervous. What in the world could possibly make Piper nervous?

"You can tell me anything," I insist and I mean that. I want to hear everything Piper has to say. She trembles a little and now I'm worried. What could be so bad?

# CHAPTER TWENTY

Piper

"I'm a virgin," I whisper as I close my eyes because I am too mortified to admit that out loud and look at him while I do it.

When I peek up at him, I find that he hasn't moved. He doesn't blink. Heck, I don't think he's even breathing.

"Kasen?" I say.

He steps back a little as if I'm made of glass and he's afraid he'll break me. Damn it!

"Stop," I say loudly. "Don't do that. Don't disappear because I shared that with you. It's not a big deal. It's a mere product of not dating. It's not some sacred thing to me." I pause but he still doesn't come closer.

Sighing, I step toward him. "I shouldn't have told you that. Two of the guys I went out with, I told that to and I never heard from them again. What is it about being a virgin that terrifies men? Seriously. I just want to get it over with." I pause, sighing again. "Maybe I should just hire a professional." And for the first time, I mean it. I'm tired of this. I'm tired of feeling like this is some weird social albatross. I'm tired of feeling like this is one of the key things that keeps me from dating men. After the second time of a guy being weird about it, I just started to retract myself from the dating world. It became that final nail in my dating-life coffin.

I'm about to tell him to just forget it. Forget the whole stupid dating-coach thing, forget that third pretend date. I'll leave a few days early. Aunt Cornelia is pretty much back to being able to get around with just Margie's help.

"Like hell you will," he growls, stopping my thoughts in their tracks. I look into his eyes and I see a fire raging. Why is he so angry? It's not *his* virginity.

I put my hands on my hips. "If you won't do it, then I *will* do it. I'm an adult. I can make these decisions for myself. Hell, I've been making decisions for myself for years. My dad pretty much checked out of parenting after the divorce. He treated me as an equal instead of a child. I was just some temporary roommate when I visited. And my mother...well, as much as she provided for me, she spent equal or great parts of her time trying to chase after God knows what in these stupid long-distance marathons. Everything about my life was centered around when she had her next race. And if she had time left over, then great, she'd be there to mom me, but I was just an afterthought, second best to first place running."

My voice shakes a little on that last statement. I've never been the most important. "I was just a check box on their life list," I whisper.

Kasen's big hands come up to my face, cupping it gently. His thumbs wipe tears that I didn't know were running down my cheeks.

"You deserve to be someone's only check box. If your parents are too blind to see how important you are, then that's their loss," he says as his eyes search mine. "You are the biggest prize, the only prize. I'm sorry they made you feel that way."

A watery laugh escapes my lips. "You're sorry? You didn't do anything wrong, Kasen. If anything, you've shown me more compassion in these last weeks than anyone has in a long time. You saw me for who I am and never questioned me, not once. And I'll always be grateful to you for that." I place a hand over his and lean into the feel of his rough palm on my cheek. "Thank you."

"You don't have to thank me." He lets out a long breath. "You saw me. And I don't think I've been seen in a long time. So I should be thanking you."

I roll my eyes. "You are a stubborn man. You know, if you just put yourself out there once in a while, you'd be seen by a whole lot more people. Don't let your parents' death, and whatever else happened to you, cause you to lock yourself away. You deserve love, Kasen. You are worthy of love."

He leans his head down so our foreheads touch and our breaths mingle. We both close our eyes. I can feel our hearts beating as one. I've never felt so connected to another human. In this single moment, I feel as if we are one being. How can I feel so entwined with him after only a few weeks? I should run away. I should leave. My fight-or-flight instincts battle with my desire to stay right here in this moment.

"OK," he whispers as he presses a kiss to my forehead and steps back.

"OK?" I furrow my brows in confusion. "OK, what?"

"I'll be your first. But only because I want you to have it done right. I don't want some guy going through the motions because you paid him or some guy doing it because he's horny after a first date. You deserve more than that, better than that, Piper. I'll do it. But we're doing this my way. If you want me to be your first, then you do as I say. If anything is uncomfortable or you change your mind, you tell me, but we do this my way," he grunts, his voice dangerously low as if it's projecting his determination.

"Your way?" I ask, raising an eyebrow.

He nods. "What were your earliest fantasies about how you'd lose it?" he asks.

I blush. "I'm not telling you that," I squeak. He has to be kidding. That shit is personal.

"If you want to do it, then you have to be willing to talk about it. Or no deal," he states as he crosses his arms, making his biceps bulge. Crap, why does this man have to be so attractive without even trying?

I roll my eyes again. "Fine. I wanted to be in love and have, like, a room full of rose petals, dimmed lighting, maybe, like, candles or something, and..." Now my face is full-on red like I-spent-all-day-at-the-beach-with-no-sunscreen red.

"And?" He looks at me, not showing even the tiniest bit of embarrassment.

"And, he takes his time until I'm...you know...ready...and then he's...gentle," I whisper, closing my eyes because I'm mortified that I just shared that aloud.

"OK, that's good. Thank you for telling me," he says as I pry my eyes back open. He doesn't look turned off at all, if anything, he looks like he wants to devour me right now.

I step back as if I'm Little Red Riding Hood and he's the Big Bad Wolf. "Y-you're welcome," I manage. I clear my throat and look back at the pot I was painting. I admit to myself that it's not half bad as I stare at it. "I should finish up here," I say as I nod toward my artwork.

He steps aside, and as I walk past him, his hand comes up and grabs my upper arm, tugging me back against him, my back to his front. He envelops me in a hug and I place my hands over his arms that are crossed over my chest. His chin presses on the crown of my head.

"For what it's worth, illustrator, and as bad as this sounds,

I'm so very glad Cornelia broke her ankle because if that hadn't happened, I'm not sure we would have met. And meeting you...well, you're helping me see some things that I've needed to see for quite a while now," he says, the hot air of his breath blowing along the shell of my ear as he speaks.

"Then, I'm glad too, not that she broke her ankle, but that I could help you." I turn in his arms and look up at him, running my fingers over the scar above his eye. "You deserve to be loved too, Kasen. I know you don't believe that, but you do. You're a good person. I see how you help your friends, and how you care about the people in this building. No matter what you've done in life, you aren't a bad person. I hope you'll believe that someday," I say as I turn and run my fingers through his thick coarse hair. His eyelids shut slowly as he lets me touch him. There's something special about this man letting me in, letting me be close to him that feels like I've tamed a wild animal. It's truly like he's a lone wolf and I just got accepted into a pack that is comprised of only the two of us.

# CHAPTER TWENTY-ONE

Kasen

I don't know what it was about spending an hour discussing my darkest, worst moments with a stranger and then telling one of them to Piper, but I wake up feeling renewed. And then I remember that I have to plan the perfect third date and...shit, I need help with this one.

A smile comes to my lips as I recall that it's men's book-club night. Yes, this one will take a village. I'd never normally go to the guys for dating advice, but I absolutely cannot fuck this up.

So, I grab a protein shake, hit the gym, and then spend my day attempting to focus on a project for a client's new server. When I finish, I shovel down some cold pizza and head to the bookstore.

Hutch and Bray are sitting in the corner, sipping beers and debating whether girls prefer licking or sucking nipples.

"I'm sorry, what?" I ask as I sit down on a chair opposite them.

"Oh, in the book we read, you read it, right?" Hutch asks.

I nod but don't elaborate or tell them I read ten others. I feel like my reputation would be ruined if they found out. Or would it? I had no idea the guys were this into romance novels.

"Well, you know that one scene in the kitchen?" Bray asks.

"Uh, yeah, sure," I state as I try to remember it.

"He sucked on her nipples, and then in a scene later, he licked them, but the character really didn't explain which felt better, so now we're discussing what we think," Hutch elaborates.

"Isn't it...subjective?" Gray asks as he walks into the back of the store.

"I mean, sure, but...Roxy, we need input," Hutch calls out and Roxy walks over from the front desk.

"Guys, I'm not Dr. Ruth. Please try out whatever you like on your own partners and then ask their preference or ask their preference first, even better," she says with a roll of her eyes. "Now, can we talk actual plot?"

Everyone grabs a drink and we set up in our book club corner. I'm not nearly as weirded out as the last time I came to this, but it still feels a bit awkward. I decide I need to get over feeling self-conscious and just get their opinion. I hate feeling this way. I've worked hard my entire adulthood to appear calm, cool, and collected, to never need any help.

"Can I ask a question?" I say, raising my hand, then dropping it immediately because I feel stupid.

"Of course, Kasen," Roxy says with a warm smile. "I'm glad you're joining us again."

OK, now this does feel like group therapy.

Pushing aside my feelings, I sit down and turn to everyone. "Can we, uh, talk about the dynamic of the relationship in the book?"

"Sure. Did you like the story?" Roxy asks as she picks up a wineglass and pours herself some more.

"I did. I wasn't so sure about the age-gap part and the part where she was his goddaughter was a little weird, but I ended up really liking it," I state as I look around. The other guys nod their agreement.

"I wasn't sure if the way he chose to take her virginity was realistic," I say as I recall a scene about it and how frenzied they were to be with each other physically.

"Weren't you in a frenzy your first time?" Hutch says with a laugh.

Roxy looks around at all of us. "Did you all lose your virginity in high school?" she asks. We all nod except Bray.

We turn to look at our friend. "Freshman year of college," he says with a shrug. I can tell Hutch was unaware of that but I had known this after Bray told me three drinks into a guys' night a few years ago.

"So, you probably were more focused on your pleasure. How many of you lost it to another virgin, like your first girlfriend or something?" Roxy asks.

Hutch and Gray raise their hands. My high school girlfriend had a boyfriend before me, and I know Bray's college girlfriend had dated before him.

"What? I'm missing virgin talk!" Drew says from the door.

I groan. "We're talking about the plot," I say with a clenched jaw.

"Oh, I mean, I thought it was pretty realistic," he says with a shrug.

I turn to him. "When did you lose your virginity?" I ask.

"Damn, Kase! Let me have a drink first," he says with a smirk.

I glare at him as he pours himself some of Roxy's wine and sits down next to her. "Believe it or not, I didn't come out till college. I dated one girl in high school and we were each other's first."

I raise an eyebrow. I hadn't known that about Drew, but then again, like a dick friend, I never asked him.

"OK, we're talking about the virginity aspect of the book, and I think Kasen had questions," Roxy offers as she motions for me to continue.

"Do you guys ever think about if you had to do it over, what would you do differently?" I ask.

There's silence for a few seconds. And I wonder if my friends can see through me. Do they know I'm about to sleep with Piper? No, they wouldn't, would they?

"Well, I wish I had been more attentive and not so rushed," Bray says with a shrug.

"Shit, I think we all feel that way. I wish I had lasted longer than thirty seconds," Hutch says with a laugh.

"Same," Gray says.

"I wish I hadn't imagined my best friend the entire time," Drew winces.

"Damn, Drew, that's fucked up," Gray says as we all laugh awkwardly.

"Yeah, it sort of was, but the guy turned out to be a prick, so I suppose I dodged a bullet with that," he adds with a shrug.

There are some grunts of understanding from the other guys. A silence follows as we all take sips of our drinks.

"I think," Roxy begins and she has our full attention. "That a woman wants to feel special. So, the main character probably just wanted her love interest to treat her like she was the most precious and important thing in his life. And he did, in his own way, so I guess that's what counts."

I half listen for the rest of the night as Roxy's words reverberate around my brain. *A woman wants to feel special. She wants*

*to be treated like she is the most precious and important thing in his
life.*

Even after the book club ends and I'm back in bed, I don't
read, I just lie there thinking of what I can do to make Piper
feel special.

It's around three in the morning that the idea hits me, and
after I carefully plan out Saturday's date, I fall asleep, where
dreams of a gorgeous woman with different-colored eyes have
me wishing Piper was here in my bed now.

———

I knock on Cornelia's door and Piper answers it. After
making sure Cornelia would be alright without her, I told her
we were going to have an overnight adventure. She is standing
there in thick tights, a short skirt, boots, and a sweater that
hangs off her shoulder. Her long hair falls in waves down her
back. She's fucking gorgeous. Her lips are glossy and it draws
my eye to them.

"You ready?" I confirm after taking her in for a beat.

"Yep, let's roll," she answers. "Bye, ladies. Behave!"

"You kids have fun," Cornelia yells.

"Hope you're taking her somewhere good," Margie says
from the kitchen.

"I am. She deserves a night away and I guarantee she will
enjoy it," I say as I wink at Piper and she turns beet red.

"She does. She's been such an angel," Cornelia says with a
sigh. "I don't know what I'd do without her."

"Oh, Aunt Cornelia, you know I'd do anything to help
you," Piper says, and I see her eyes mist over. I had no idea
that her great-aunt meant that much to her, but it's evident
now as I watch her reaction to the kind words.

"I know, sweetheart. Now, go have fun," Cornelia replies,

and I swear I hear emotion in her voice, which is very un-Cornelia-like.

I hold out my hand and Piper takes it. Shaking my head, I motion for her bag. She hands it to me and I sling it over my shoulder and then hold out my other hand. She entwines her fingers with mine. I rub my thumb over the smooth skin on the palm of her hand as we walk out to my waiting car.

"Are you going to tell me where we're going?" she asks.

I shake my head. "It's a surprise."

I open the car door for her and she gets in as I lean toward her. "There's only one rule. If you don't like something this weekend, you have to promise to tell me, OK?"

"OK," she whispers, her big multicolored eyes searching mine.

"Good," I state as I close her door and walk around the car, tossing her bag in the back with mine as I hop into the driver's seat.

I drive us out of the city a ways until we reach the exit for our location. The roads narrow and there's hardly another car. We finally come up on a giant farm property. There's a vineyard in front, but it's the building in the back that I stop at and park.

"Where are we?" she asks.

I walk around the car and open her door. She exits and looks around us.

"Come on, I have arranged for an activity before dinner," I explain as I motion for her to follow me into the building.

We enter and she gasps. I may have had to pull a few strings, but in the end, the look on her face is worth every conversation I was forced to have for the last seventy-two hours.

"I...what?" she stammers as she looks around us.

A man crosses the room and extends his hand. "Ms. Dawson, I'm so pleased to have you join me tonight. Mr.

Saddler said you are looking to illustrate books. So, I offered a lesson," he says. "I'm Buckley Sullivan, but please, call me Sully."

"Y-you're, like, wow. It's so nice to meet you, Mr. Sullivan, I mean, Sully," she stumbles over her words as she releases his hand.

"Have a seat. This is a lesson for two," he says with a grin. He's set up two canvases in front of one for him.

And just like that, one of the world's most famous children's book illustrators gives us a private lesson on his farm. He praises and encourages Piper and I'm so grateful that Al offered to call his old friend.

"Thank you, Sully. This has been a dream come true," Piper gushes as we wrap up our lesson.

"Happy to have met you, Piper. Here's a card with my number and email, feel free to reach out anytime," he says and then points toward the road we drove in on. "I think the guesthouse is all ready with dinner when you are."

"Dinner?" Piper asks.

"Yeah, when my wife wanted to buy this place, I had no idea the plans she had for it. She and my daughters run the vineyard, and last year, they put two guesthouses out by the lake. But you're the only ones out there tonight. We were going to close them for the season, but Al talked me into taking one last booking. My daughter Jessica is a great chef, she's prepared your dinner on the veranda."

"Thanks again, Sully," I say as I shake his hand.

He waves at us. "I'll have Martha drop these on the front steps of the cabin tomorrow before checkout."

I nod and place my hand on the small of Piper's back, ushering her back to the car. I drive us a mile down the road where it ends at a lake. There's an A-frame building and another one a little further down the path.

I park in the nearest one where I can see a candlelit table on a deck overlooking the water.

"Holy shit, Kasen. This is amazing," Piper says excitedly as she gets out of the car before I can open the door for her.

She's already walking to the deck.

I jump out and take her hand, dragging her back against me. "Slow down there, illustrator. Let's get our stuff and then we'll change for dinner." I had told her to pack a nice outfit.

She nods and I take our bags. We get settled in the house. Everything we need is there. The loft master suite looks out over the lake. It really is gorgeous.

"Go ahead and change. I'll meet you on the deck," I say. She nods and heads into the bathroom. I throw on a suit and walk downstairs, stopping in the kitchen to grab the ice bucket with the champagne inside and two champagne flutes.

I set them on the table outside and take a seat to wait.

A moment later, Piper walks out onto the deck, and I nearly stop breathing. She's beyond beautiful. Her hair is pinned up on top of her head. Tendrils hang down her long neck. She's wearing makeup and her lips are bright red. She has on a red dress that hugs every curve on her body.

*Fuck me.*

"I sort of was hoping that is what you would do to me," she says with a smirk.

I realize I said those words out loud and I grin. "That's the plan," I reply.

I stand and hold out a hand. She takes it and I twirl her in a circle. She giggles.

"You're stunning," I manage.

"Thank you," she says quietly.

I pull out her chair and she sits.

"Let's eat and enjoy the evening," I say, but I'm not sure I can, because all I want to do is take her up to that giant king-sized bed and make her mine. I want to ruin her for every other man forever. And that thought both makes me terrified and also exceedingly happy all at once.

# CHAPTER TWENTY-TWO

Piper

Everything about the evening seems perfect. We eat delicious food and talk about everything and nothing all at the same time. I make Kasen tell me a story about growing up and fishing with his dad. He smiles as he tells the story. He becomes less and less mysterious over the course of the meal, and by the time he's feeding me chocolate cake, I'm trying to tell myself I'm not falling for him.

I pat my stomach as I sit back in my chair and stare up at the night sky. We're a good two hours from the city and you can see so many more stars here.

"You want to walk down to the water?" he asks as he points to the dock at the end of a path from the deck. It's lit up with little solar lights on either side of the pebble trail.

"Sure. I could use a little walk," I state as I get up and link arms with him. We walk down to the end of the dock. I take my shoes off and set them beside me. It's unseasonably warm tonight, but I still shiver a little.

He pulls me against him, wrapping his arm around my shoulder.

"You want to dance, illustrator?" he asks.

I frown. "There's no music," I point out and he pulls his phone out and plays an old song I heard my grandmother playing once.

He takes me in his arms, and we dance. I feel like I'm at prom, something I never went to. It's like life is giving me a do-over.

"What are you thinking?" he inquires as we sway back and forth.

"I never went to prom," I explain. "And this sort of feels like life is making up for it."

He presses a kiss on my forehead. "I'm glad. You deserve every experience."

"Every experience?" I ask, my voice teasing.

He chuckles. "Yes, every last one."

I lean up and plant a kiss on his lips. It's not meant to be sexy, but somewhere between a sweet kiss and his arms wrapped tightly around me, it changes. The air crackles between us and Kasen reaches down and lifts me into his arms, bridal-style. We continue kissing as he walks us back up to the house and straight into the bedroom.

When he sets me down, I'm dizzy with need, and I grasp on to him for support.

"Slow down," he says gently. "We have all night."

"OK," I say as I stop moving, unsure of what to do.

"We need to get you out of your head. How about we take a bath? There's a giant hot tub in the bathroom," he suggests.

"I didn't bring a bathing suit," I say and then shut my mouth immediately because I realize he means we take a bath with no clothes.

"Are you OK with that?" he asks, seemingly reading my mind.

My mouth is dry but I nod. It's time to rip off this bandage.

He motions for me to turn around with his finger and I comply. He slowly pulls the zipper of my dress down and holds it open so I can step out of it. I'm left in my underwear and his eyes become hooded as he takes me in.

"May I?" I ask as I point to his tie. He nods and I remove his tie and push his suit jacket off his shoulders. He wriggles out of it as it bunches at his biceps. Then I remove his white button-down shirt and his belt buckle. I fumble with the button of his pants, my hands shaking a little.

"There's not a rush," he assures me as he places his hand over mine. I take a breath and release the button, pushing down the zipper and watching as his pants fall away. He reaches down and removes them with his socks.

Now we're both left in our underwear. I walk into the bathroom and he follows. He fills the hot tub and turns on the jets.

As he goes to dim the lights, I quickly remove my bra and underwear and begin sinking into the warm, bubbling water. I groan at the feeling of it. I open my eyes to see Kasen watching me.

"You coming in?" I ask as I start to turn to give him privacy.

"You can watch me," he offers. I stay put and my eyes drop to where he's hooked his thumbs in the elastic waistband of his underwear. I'm not sure what I expect. I've seen a few penises before, but I'm not prepared for Kasen's.

My eyes widen at the sight of him. My brain does mental gymnastics as I attempt to figure out how the enormous appendage between his legs is going to fit inside me.

He tosses his underwear to the side and climbs into the tub.

We sit at opposite sides until he reaches out and pulls me

toward him. My legs go to the outside of his, and as I sit, I feel his hard length pressed against my center. Holy shit! This is actually happening.

His eyes search mine. "I went to the doctor this week and got bloodwork, just to make sure I'm good to go. I am," he assures me.

"Can we..." I trail off unsure of how to ask him this question.

He presses a finger under my chin and I look back into his eyes. "I've been taking the pill for a year or so because of my cramps."

"What do you want, baby? Use your words and tell me. Tonight is all about me making you feel good," he coaxes.

"No...barriers," I say.

"Shit, I...OK. I've only done that a few other times with my last girlfriend," he explains.

I nod and relax a little. "Good, then it puts us more on equal footing since it'll be sort of a newish thing for both of us."

He pushes a strand of hair back behind my ear and follows the path of his finger with his lips. "You make me feel like everything is new all the time, Piper. I'm not sure I actually saw the world before I met you."

I moan as he sucks lightly on my neck, my head tipping to the side to give him more access. He grips my ass and I start moving against him. The water sloshes against the sides of the tub. I'm only half aware of the mess I'm making as the waves reach over the edge and water hits the floor.

All of a sudden, he stands and I squeal, wrapping my legs around his waist.

He grabs two towels and uses one to dry us off and the other he lays across the bed after he yanks the comforter down. I slide down his body and he finishes making sure I'm dry everywhere but between my legs.

Stepping back, he looks at me. His face is a myriad of emotions. I shiver under his gaze and he motions for me to get in bed. Then he pushes a pillow under the towel and settles my ass on top of it. I'm elevated slightly and feel so exposed. He's kneeling between my legs and I wonder if this is it. Am I about to lose my virginity?

"Not yet, baby. Let me get you ready," he says in a low gravelly voice as he leans down and pushes my legs further apart, making room for him to lie down. His face is mere inches away from an area no man has ever explored before.

"Close your eyes and just feel," he encourages. The second my eyes are closed, I feel him run a single finger between my folds, separating them with each stroke. The way his finger easily glides along my most sensitive skin tells me how wet I am.

But apparently, I'm not wet enough because, after a few moments, he slides his finger inside me to the second knuckle, and his tongue presses to my clit. I nearly leap off the bed from the intensity of it.

"Relax," he coos as he sucks on my clit while pumping his finger slowly in and out of me. How is he so good at that? I start to contemplate the answer to that but then he flicks his tongue over that bundle of nerves and I lose track of my thoughts.

I feel myself relaxing and my legs begin to fall open as his tongue goes from my clit to my entrance and back again. After a few minutes, I'm pretty sure I'm dying. I need him inside me now. I squirm and he shooshes me.

I feel a second finger push inside me. I feel so full as he pumps deeper.

I start to grind against him, needing more, wanting more. I'm so wet that it makes a noise as he licks and sucks me. I want to be mortified, but I don't care. I'm so needy that all I can think about is Kasen being inside me. He tries for a third finger and I reach down.

"Too full," I groan as I grip his hand. His tongue licks through my fingers to reach my clit, and fuck, that was hot.

"You need me to loosen you up. I want this to be good for you," he explains as he pushes my legs wider apart with one hand while continuing to suck and lick and push his third finger into me. His fingers can barely move and it burns a little. I feel his saliva as he spits on his fingers and pushes them a little deeper.

I close my eyes and whimper when he pulls his fingers from me and gives me a final lick that ends with his tongue inside me.

"Please," I beg, not even sure what I'm begging for.

He kneels and I feel him run the head of his dick up and down my wetness until he's sliding through my inner folds and then it gets lodged at my opening. I squirm, trying to force him inside.

"Slow," he murmurs and I feel his hand guiding him inside a little bit at a time, in and out, inch by inch until he slides all the way inside causing a burning sensation. He keeps himself suspended above me with one hand. And I watch him as he looks at where we're joined.

"Fuck, you have no idea how hot you look wrapped around my cock, baby," he says.

Dirty talk. This is what it's like. And I think I'm a huge fan.

"Please, move," I plead as I squirm beneath him. It didn't hurt like in the movies, it's just uncomfortable. He's so big and I'm not sure how this will work.

"You OK?" he asks as he looks at me.

I nod. "Yes, please move."

He starts slow, and I thrust up to meet him. We find a

rhythm and he grabs my ankles and spreads my legs farther apart, completely controlling me.

"Deeper," I groan and he slams into me completely. And we both moan.

He hits some part of me that has my mind going blank. The only thing existing is him inside me and the friction our bodies are creating. He places my ankles on his shoulder and leans down, stretching my legs toward me.

"Oh!" I yelp in surprise as he slides deeper.

"You OK?" he grunts, freezing for a second.

"Yes, yes, so OK, better than OK," I murmur. He chuckles and bites my lower lip, and I moan again as he starts moving.

I didn't think an orgasm during my first time would be possible, but whatever he's doing has me flying toward a release.

"Don't stop, please don't stop," I cry out as I feel myself charging toward a high like I've never felt before. His thumb reaches between us, drawing tight circles around my clit as he thrusts inside me.

He moves faster as I begin to tremble, losing complete control of my muscles as my entire body spasms and my mouth drops open in a silent cry. My head falls back onto the pillow, and a second later, Kasen grunts and I feel the warmth spilling inside me as his cock jerks.

"Holy shit! Is that what I've been missing this whole time?" I whisper.

He presses kisses to my cheek and jaw as his cock gives one last jerk inside me and we both groan.

"I think that's what *I've* been missing. Damn you feel good," he says as he pulls out and I wince a little.

"OK?" he confirms.

I nod and he gets up and comes back with a warm wet

cloth, wiping me between my legs and then crawling up the bed. He tucks me against him and kisses my forehead, and I smile as I drift to sleep.

# CHAPTER TWENTY-THREE

Kasen

I wake first. My eyes pop open as I assess my surroundings. I realize I'm safe and I feel my heart rate slow. I look down at Piper whose chest rises and falls with each breath. Her hair is fanned out around her face and my chest.

I hope I did this right. I hope that I took care of her how she wanted me to. I haven't thought about anyone but my friends, grandmother, and myself in so long, it seems foreign to welcome a new person into my inner circle.

I felt bad when I realized she had bled a little on me. But she kept reassuring me she was fine. I could never fathom hurting her in any way. I knew last night would make her sore but damn it if I don't want to do that again and again.

The sun starts to rise and the room gets lighter. I watch as Piper stretches like a cat. It makes me smile as she snuggles closer to me, hitching her leg over mine. I press my face against the top of her head, smelling that floral shampoo that calms me.

"Good morning," she mumbles against my chest.

"Good morning," I reply, tightening my hold on her as if I'm afraid she'll get up and leave.

"You hungry?" I ask.

Her head moves and she looks up at me. "Famished!"

Chuckling, I roll us over and look down at her. Fuck, she's gorgeous. How did I get so lucky to be the one she chose? A dark thought pops into my head.

*She deserves better. She deserves all the things I can't give her. She deserves a sane boyfriend who doesn't travel all the time.*

"What? What is that face for?" Piper says sleepily as she looks up at me. I can see the cobwebs of sleep slowly fading from her eyes and I know I have to mask my inner concerns.

I bury my face in her neck and exhale, pushing all the bad thoughts away...at least for now.

"Nothing, let's make breakfast," I say as I get out of bed. I hold out my hand and she takes it, letting me pull her up and into my arms.

"How do you feel?" I ask as I look into those two different-colored eyes, two eyes that see me in a way that both scares me and intrigues me.

"A little sore, but good," she admits with a shrug and then a smirk.

"What?" I question.

"When do we have to leave here?" she asks.

"We have all day. Sully said they aren't taking any more reservations this fall, so we're the last ones," I explain.

"Good. Then we have time," she says cheerfully as she leans up and gives me a quick kiss before she scurries over to her bag and puts on an oversized T-shirt.

"What should we do for breakfast?" she adds as she looks at me over her shoulder. The light hits her hair and she looks like an angel with all the golds bouncing off her highlights.

"I had them leave a bagel tray with fruit. It's in the

kitchen," I explain as I walk out with nothing on because why the hell not.

She follows me and I go about setting the tray of bagels, some cream cheese from the refrigerator, and some fruit out on the kitchen island. I grab the orange juice and offer her some. She nods and starts cutting a bagel, placing it in the toaster. I lean back against the counter and watch as she moves around the kitchen, seemingly in her own little world. She spreads the cream cheese on her bagel and takes a bite, moaning a little as she chews. And fuck, I can't stop myself. I close the space between us in three steps, pushing myself between her legs and gripping her hips. I lift her onto the island.

Her eyes grow big as she looks up at me. Then she grins and holds out her bagel to me. I take a bite of it and then she takes a bite. We finish the half bagel quickly, our gazes remaining locked as we chew.

"That was good," she says in a low voice.

"It was. Need more?" I ask, motioning to the platter where a handful of bagels still sit.

She nods. I reach around her to grab another bagel, but her hand comes out to stop me. Her legs wrap around my waist and my cock comes to life as she presses herself against me.

"I need more, but not more bagels," she clarifies.

"Oh?" I play dumb.

She rolls her eyes and pokes my ribs. "Stop messing with me. How am I ever going to get good at this if we don't practice?"

*Oh, baby, you are a natural. You don't need a single lesson. You're already expert level.*

She pushes at my chest, and I step back in confusion. I watch as she scoots off the island and drops to her knees in front of me. Her eyes settle on my dick and she licks her lips.

*Holy fuck! That's hot!*

She looks up at me from beneath her lashes. "I...don't really know what I'm doing," she says as she purses her lips.

I take a breath and reach out, placing a hand under her chin. "Just be careful with your teeth. You can use your hand too. I'll try to be still," I offer.

She nods and I can see the excitement in her eyes. She gently wraps a hand around me and I moan as she strokes me to my base.

"Is that OK?" she whispers.

I nod and watch as she holds me in one hand and takes me in her mouth, running her tongue along the underside of my erection. She covers her teeth and takes me deep in her mouth.

"Fuck, baby, that feels good," I praise as I grip the back of her head. She doubles her efforts, licking and sucking, and then her other hand that's been on my thigh moves to cup my balls.

"Baby, I'm going to come. If you don't want me to come in your mouth, you need to..." I pause as she pushes me farther back toward her throat. "Fuck," I say slowly as I feel my balls tighten and I come with one thrust in her mouth.

She swallows it all and then licks my length as she pulls away. I shudder from the overstimulation as she caresses my balls one final time.

She places her hands on her thighs and looks up at me. "Was that...OK?"

I don't have words. I don't have thoughts. I'm pretty sure I've lost the capacity to think. So, I fall to my knees, take her face in my hands, and kiss her, tasting myself on her tongue and not caring one bit.

I pour every emotion I'm feeling into that kiss. I can't speak the words, but I can show her. I can tell her this is so much more than playing pretend. What I'm feeling for her is real. As much as I don't want it to be, as much as I want to protect her from me, I'm not sure I'm strong enough to do that.

When I pull back, her eyes remain closed. Her lips are swollen and wet. I can't help but give them one final kiss.

"Is it always like this?" she asks as her eyes open.

"No, it's not always like this. It's not always this perfect," I say because that's the truth.

I stand and pull her up with me. "Let's shower."

I lead her up to the master suite and turn on the shower. I take my time, washing her hair and soaping her body. I memorize each line and crease, every freckle and hair. And then I let her wash me. She has to stand on the shower seat to reach my hair. Her giggles have me pulling her against me and pressing kisses all over her face and breasts.

"Stop," she says with laughter. "Let me wash your hair!"

I step back and let her continue. When we're clean, rinsed, and towel-dried, I lead her out to the dock. We sit down and look out over the lake. She leans her head on my shoulder and I feel so at peace.

"I wish we could stay here longer," she says after a few minutes.

"Me too," I admit.

"Maybe we can come back here someday," she says and I'm not sure if she really means it or if she's just trying to be nice.

"Perhaps we will," I state, not knowing what else to say.

"Did you always like the water as a kid?" she asks. I consider her question for a few seconds, but it's one memory in particular that makes me laugh.

She puts her head up and looks at me. "What?"

"Just remembering when my dad taught me to swim," I say as I look down at her. Her eyes are bright and curious, and something about that makes me want to share the story.

"I was maybe five and we'd gone over to visit my grandparents in Scotland. I said I wanted to go on the boat with them, but Dad said I couldn't go until I learned to swim. I asked him to teach me and he just tossed me in the water. I thought for sure I was going to die. But then he jumped in with me and held me up, he flipped me on my back and said to relax. So after a bit, I did and I floated. Right as I was starting to get the hang of it, a dolphin came into the cove and we stayed there and swam with it. Well, I sort of clung to Dad but we'd stick our heads under and it'd come over to us. And after that, I was just...hooked. I always wanted to be in the water or around the water. Even after they died and after the explosion on the beach, I never stopped wanting to be in the water."

"Explosion?" Piper asks, pulling her knees up to her face and setting her chin on them as she wraps her arms around her legs, making her seem so small.

I look back out at the water. "I was in a special ops unit. We had come in from the water. We were supposed to scout an area along the shore. My friend was next to me. I went left and he went right. There was an old landmine to the right. We had been told the area was cleared and...well, it wasn't." I point to the scar on my forehead, the one on my side, and my leg. "I got cut up pretty bad. Tyler lost his life."

"I'm sorry," she says, reaching out a hand and grabbing mine. "Is that when you got out of the military?"

I nod. "I lost some hearing in my right ear, and between the physical stuff and the PTSD, they honorably discharged me."

"And then what?" she asks.

"I went to college. I'd worked on some computer stuff in the military and liked it. My former commander suggested I study cybersecurity and, well, he was right. I did love it and I was good at it. A guy I knew from my early days in the Navy had started a firm and I began working for him. Eventually, I got too good and now I consult, which is nice. I set my own hours, pick my own projects, and basically dictate when and where I want to work most of the time. He's still the boss and sometimes I have to take projects that I don't want, but being a contract employee does give me more flexibility." I stop speaking, realizing how much I've been saying. It's the most I've told anyone in a long time.

"It sounds nice, working solo but still being part of a team," she says.

"Maybe you can do it too," I suggest.

"Maybe," she answers. She turns to me. "Do you think we have time to...practice some stuff again before we leave?"

I laugh at her subject change. "Yes, illustrator, I think we have time to practice." I pick her up and she yelps as I toss her over my shoulder and walk her up to the house.

"Kasen! Put me down!" she giggles as she slaps my ass.

I only put her down once we get to the bedroom. She looks up at me.

"Practice makes perfect," she says, and with that, I help her practice two more times.

# CHAPTER TWENTY-FOUR

Piper

"Oh my God! It's a Dairy Queen! Can we stop?" I say excitedly as we drive toward the interstate.

"Please tell me it's because you need a Blizzard," Kasen says as he pulls into the parking lot.

"Obviously," I answer because who doesn't love Blizzards.

We get out and go inside to order. I look at the flavor of the month but decide to go with my staple, Oreo.

"I'll have the same," Kasen says and I grin.

We get our ice cream and sit on a bench outside to eat it.

"What's your favorite food?" I ask because this ice cream thing is making me think that I really don't know this man, and after what we've done in the past twenty-four hours, I probably should get to know him a little better.

I watch him lick the ice cream off his spoon and memories of his tongue on me earlier today have me pressing my thighs together.

"That's a tough one," he says as he eats his Blizzard. I take another bite of mine and wait for him to contemplate it.

"I mean, I love fish and chips, but I think…this is going to sound weird"—he pauses and looks at me—"corn dogs."

I giggle. "No way."

"Way."

I roll my eyes. "I love corn dogs, but like the type you get at a fair. It has to be legit."

He grins and I realize how sexy he looks grinning. He is serious so much of the time. "Exactly. That's how I feel about it."

"When did you have your first corn dog?" I ask.

"The county fair. I was maybe five or six. I also had funnel cake," he says.

"My grandmother took me to the state fair when I was eight. My mom never used to buy hot dogs or any junk food because she was always training for a race. So I ate my weight in all the food. I remember feeling so sick but I didn't care," I say as I finish my ice cream.

"Did you spend a lot of time with your grandparents when you were a kid?" he asks.

Nodding, I toss my cup and spoon away. "My mom's mom and dad lived nearby, so I spent a fair amount of time with them. I only saw my dad's parents once a year. What about you?"

"Well, I didn't get to see my grandparents very often because they lived in Scotland and Key West," he says.

"Key West as in Florida?" I ask.

He nods. "Yeah. My mom's parents lived down there. They were in their early forties when she was born and she was a bit of a surprise baby. My aunt and uncle are fifteen and sixteen years older than her. I hear from them once in a while but her parents died when I was maybe seven or eight. My dad was a twin but his brother died two days after they were born. I have cousins on that side of the family but I've only met them once or twice. My dad wasn't very close with his siblings." He pauses and then continues. "And then Granddad died about eight years ago. So it's just me and my grandmother."

He finishes his ice cream and tosses the cup in the trash. We climb back into his car and head back toward the city.

It's amazing how much we have in common. We like the same bands, a lot of the same movies, and he even admitted to liking a reality television series that is my total guilty pleasure.

By the time we pull up to one-eleven Hearts Lane, I feel like I know a completely different Kasen than the one I met in the hallway several weeks ago. He comes around to my side and opens my door and helps me out, slinging my bag over his shoulder.

"What about your stuff?" I ask as I point to his bag in the back of the car.

"I'll get it later," he says as he places his hand on the small of my back and steers me toward the building.

We stop when we hear Hutch yell out, "God damn it!"

I turn to see Hutch throwing something on the ground and stomping toward us.

"Whoa. What's going on?" Kasen asks.

"The freaking trash pandas is what's going on," Hutch growls throwing his hands up in exasperation.

"I'm sorry, what?" I ask in confusion. Kasen pulls me protectively to his side.

"Bro, did the fuzzy little bears mess up another trail cam?" Kasen asks.

"Mess it up? Hardly. They massacred it. They completely annihilated it. That's the third one they've killed," he grumbles.

I really do try to be serious. I fight the laugh bubbling up in my throat. But a giggle makes its way out of my mouth.

Hutch glares at me and I clamp a hand over my lips. "Sorry," I mumble behind my fingers.

Kasen's body shakes with silent laughter.

"Dude, those things are expensive. It's not funny," Hutch says as he glares at us.

"I'm sorry, Hutch. It's just...why do you keep putting out trail cams if the raccoons keep messing with them?" I ask.

"Well, Hutch here is determined to find out who puts flowers out on the bench over there every morning. So far, he hasn't cracked the case," Kasen explains.

Hutch shrugs. "It's sort of become my hobby."

"The bench where I paint?" I ask.

Hutch's interest is piqued. "What are you painting?"

I nod. "I paint the lily pads in the little pond next to the stream," I explain as I point in the direction of the bench. "And frogs sometimes."

"You should talk to Roxy. She mentioned trying to help her author friend do some book art," Hutch suggests.

"Already did. Not sure if anyone will ask me to do any art for them, but maybe," I state.

Kasen squeezes my arm. "They will. You're going to be a famous artist."

I roll my eyes. "Let's just start with being an artist who gets commissioned to do anything."

"Baby steps," Hutch adds.

"Exactly," I agree.

It's then that Hutch eyes the bag. "You guys going somewhere?"

"No, just coming back from visiting an artist," Kasen says quickly. I wonder if he's embarrassed to tell his friend about our weekend away. I mean, it's not a secret, not exactly. Maybe I should be embarrassed. After all, I can't even get a real boyfriend. I have to employ one to practice with.

I blush. "I should get upstairs and check on my aunt," I say. "Good luck with the trash pandas, Hutch."

"Thanks. It's back to the drawing board," he says. "I need coffee for this." I watch as he walks over to the café.

"Come on, illustrator. Let's get you settled," Kasen says as he guides me inside. We're both quiet as we ride the elevator, but when we get to our floor, Kasen presses the emergency button and the elevator shakes to a stop.

"W-what are you doing?" I manage to ask before he drops my bag, walks us into a wall, and picks me up. I squeal and wrap my legs around his waist as he presses me into a mirrored panel and kisses me.

I'm not sure how long we kiss for, but eventually, he pulls back. Our heavy breathing is the only sound inside the metal elevator.

"I had a good time this weekend," he says, breaking the silence.

"Same," I reply, my lips twitching with a smile. I frown a little and his brows furrow.

"What's wrong?" he asks.

I smirk. "I think I could use more practice. Are you free later tonight?"

This time his smile is so wide it nearly splits his face. "I could probably accommodate that. I mean, there's so many things we didn't practice."

My eyes widen. "Like what?" I say.

"Like, this position for instance," he says as he thrusts his groin against me. I mean, he's right, we didn't do it standing up. He's quiet for a moment. "Are you sore?"

I shake my head. It's a little bit of a white lie. I am slightly sore, but not enough to keep me from wanting more of Kasen. If I only get him for another week, I'm going to get as much of him as I can possibly have. I can't imagine a future boyfriend being better at sex than he is.

"Did you enjoy it?" he asks, his forehead pressing against mine.

"If I didn't, I wouldn't be asking for more practice, now would I?" I say.

"Good, because I think as your teacher, you need a lot more practice," he says as he leans in and kisses me again.

I grin and kiss him. "I think." Kiss. "I'm going to like." Kiss. "All this practice." Kiss.

"Your aunt can wait. You need another lesson right now," Kasen says as he releases the emergency button, grabs my bag, and carries me out and straight into his apartment. I think I like having a pretend boyfriend. But right now, Kasen feels more real than any other guy I've ever dated. Will I be able to let him go in a week?

# CHAPTER TWENTY-FIVE

Kasen

"Kasen, can you have the firewall sorted by Tuesday?" my boss asks. This is the fourth project he's offered me this week, and like a dumbass, I've agreed to take it on. I know he's down employees and I was gone for a while, but I've about reached my limit.

"Colden, that's going to be a tight timeline. Do they need it by Tuesday?" I question as I look at the progress of my other three projects.

"Unfortunately they do. You're my best at this. I know I've loaded you with work this week, but business is booming," Colden explains.

Sighing, I rub a hand over my face. I'm going to need to triple my caffeine intake and I will probably need to miss one of my gym sessions. I grimace at what else I'll be missing. Maybe I can get Piper to come sleep here? Then at least I can help her practice.

*Practice.* Who am I kidding? I don't know what changed

out at the lake house, but something is different. I know Piper's leaving in less than a week, but I just can't accept that. Can I?

"Dude, you still there?" Colden says.

"Yeah, I'll do my best," I say and immediately regret it.

"Thanks, I appreciate this. I'll double your bonus if you get it done on time," he adds.

"Yeah, yeah. I gotta go," I say as I disconnect. I really need more coffee before I dive into this. I finish up one test on my coding I worked on all morning and then I head over to get coffee.

It's nice outside as I cross over to the café. A small part of me wishes I could work outside but my secure setup doesn't allow that.

"Kasen, you OK?" Cam asks after I order my usual.

"I'm fine. Just swamped," I explain.

"OK. Remember to hydrate," Cam scolds as she hands me water and a coffee.

I nod and hurry back to my office. Putting on the headphones, I get down to work on the assignment. Somehow, I lose track of time. I realize the day has passed when my only light is coming from the one on my desk.

Rubbing my eyes, I pull off my headphones and decide to order takeout. It's late but the moon is bright as I walk down the street to Joe's Tavern, a local hangout. I order a burger and fries and then sit outside and wait. I have so much to do that even taking an hour off seems stressful. My mind drifts to Piper.

What would dating her for real be like? She'd want to eat dinner with me, probably. And date nights and movie nights and a lot of sex.

I frown. I don't have room in my life for Piper. Sure, we'd be all over each other for a few weeks, but then what?

I'd be busy with work. She'd be trying to figure out life.

I'm more settled and she's starting out. She'd want all the attention she deserves, and I can't give her that all the time.

"Kasen?" the hostess's voice rings out from the door. I turn and she hands me my dinner in a box.

"Thanks," I mutter and head home. If I wasn't feeling bogged down before, I am now. I eat in silence in my apartment, still trying to figure out a way that it could work with Piper, but by my last fry, I know there's no hope for us. We are too different and I am too busy and emotionally fucked up to give her what she needs.

I wish she was leaving today. I could rip off the bandage and just get on with life.

But even as I think that, I find myself thinking, "It could work! You could be happy!"

I'm too afraid to believe those words, but they are there, brewing alongside thoughts of being too old and too busy.

---

"How's Piper?" Al asks as he stands by the coffee machine, waiting for Cam to make his drink.

"She's fine, I guess. I've only texted her this week. I'm swamped at work," I explain.

"Oh? Well, you should take a night off. I was going to throw her a little going-away party later since she'll miss happy hour on Thursday. I didn't see you check in on the group chat, so make sure to check your text messages later," Al says. He's right. I haven't looked at my phone in hours.

I swallow a lump in my throat. I've been putting off thinking about Piper leaving. I know she booked a plane ticket from here directly to Seattle. Part of me thinks this is for the best. A clean break before I get too attached and likely ruin things between us. Another part of me is screaming to stop her from leaving, but I push that thought back deep into the recesses of my brain.

Deciding to switch topics, I turn back to Cam. "Any word on you buying this place?" I ask.

She smiles and nods. "I met with Phyllis, the owner, and we have an agreement on a transition plan, and yesterday," she says, then turns to Al and says, "Drum roll, please."

Al gives a drum roll.

"I got approved for my small business loan!" she says excitedly as she claps her hands. "I was going to tell everyone at happy hour, but who am I kidding. I'm way too excited to keep that shit to myself."

"Wow! That's great news!" Al says.

"Congratulations. That's wonderful news," I add.

"Thank you both. Prepare to taste test a ton of baked goods and new coffees! Drew and I have been spending every night coming up with ideas," she says with a grin.

"Well"—Al pats his stomach—"we all know I'm an excellent taste tester."

Cam giggles and hands Al his drink and then hands me mine. "Don't forget the water," she calls out after me as she passes me a bottled water. Something she's now begun to do with every coffee purchase I make.

Al motions to the water as we exit. "What's up with the added hydration?" he asks.

I groan. "I've been having to double up with caffeine lately. Work has been crazy busy. I'm debating whether or not I'll even have time to be on-site for the project that I've been wrapping up. I was going to fly over to Berlin and meet with the team in person, but I don't think I'll be able to make it work. I need my setup here to complete the other projects."

Al pats my back. "Kasen, you need a break, my friend. You work too hard all the time. I know you love your work but maybe take a few days off. There's a whole world out here." He pauses and points to the park. "Piper has an uncanny ability to see the world through a different lens. She's brought life back to our greenhouse and I just commissioned her to finish a set of lily pad and frog paintings for me."

"You did?" I ask.

He nods. "Her artwork is phenomenal. Edith would love it," he says sadly. Now it's me who pats him on the back. Just like everyone in the building, we all miss his wife. She was like the grandmother figure and wise friend that everyone needed. "My poker friend's wife owns an art gallery, I'm trying to see if she'll show some of Piper's art."

My heart lurches at the thought of her having her art in a local gallery. Would she move here? I quickly squash that idea. I need to stop trying to keep Piper as mine. She deserves someone who isn't so mentally messed up.

"That's great," I reply, attempting to sound enthusiastic.

Al turns to me as we reach the door to the building.

"Kasen, let me give you a little advice. I know there's some song about a man being a rock or an island or something, but you are not an island. I know your life has had its challenges, but don't block people because of that. Do I miss Edith? Yes, every damn day. Would I give up the years I had with her because of how sad I have been since she died? Hell no. I'm thankful for every minute I had with her. She made me better and she made my life better. Consider that," he says as he lets go of my arm that he's grabbed. He motions toward the park and I see Piper painting in her usual spot on the bench.

I nod, unable to answer because of the swell of emotion rising in my throat.

"Good." He tips his hat and walks inside, leaving me standing there staring at Piper as she paints. She has on headphones and the protector in me is mad at her for not paying attention to her surroundings. I walk toward her without thought, as if we're magnets that are trying to connect. I feel lighter the closer I get to her. She's like a planet of happiness and I'm getting sucked into her gravitational pull.

I'm surprised when she looks up at me before I've even gotten within two feet of her.

She smiles and pulls off her headphones. "Hey," she says cheerfully.

"Hey," I reply. I nod toward the painting she's working on. "Looks good."

"Sort of. I want to try a new technique on the flowers. I'm just debating if I'll do it on this one or start another," she says with a frown as she sizes up her work.

Al didn't say if he'd told her yet about the art gallery, so I don't say anything. I just stand there, looking at her painting. It's calming. A brief thought of her in my grandmother's den flashes before me. There's a big picture window there that looks out over the mountains and the sunrise. She'd love it.

Her phone pings and she reads a message. She looks up and sees me trying to read over her shoulder.

"It's my dad. We're trying to work out how I'll get out to his house. He has a meeting," she says with a sigh and then shrugs. "It'll be nice to see him. We don't spend much time together."

I decide right at that moment that I need to let her go. She needs to find her own way to her dreams. She's still so young. I'm nearly ten years older than her. I've lived a thousand different lives since I was her age. It's strange to think of the age gap between us. She doesn't seem like a twenty-three-year-old.

After I make that decision, I also decide to take her on one final practice date. A goodbye date.

# CHAPTER TWENTY-SIX

Piper

"How about one more practice date?" Kasen says as I pack up my things.

"When?" I ask.

"Well, it sounds like tonight we have an impromptu happy hour," he says. "How about tomorrow night?"

He holds my bag while I place things inside and break down my easel. "Sure. What'd you have in mind?" I ask.

He shrugs. "Is there anything you wanted to do before you leave?"

I contemplate that while we begin walking back to the apartment building. "I never got to go to the new art museum that opened last summer," I suggest.

He places a hand on the small of my back and it makes me sad. I'm going to miss that. I'm going to miss him. And not just because he's good at sex or kissing or cuddling. I mean, yeah, I love those things about him, but I also will miss our conversations. I'll miss the way he protects me more than anyone else I know. I'll miss the way he loves his sea creatures. I'll miss him fixing us whiskey. I'll miss how he quietly sees the people around him and helps them without even being asked.

Kasen Saddler is the real deal. I guess I shouldn't be sad. I should be happy to have had a man like him willing to help me learn how to date and to have lost my "v" card to a man who knew exactly how to touch me. But I can't shake this sadness. I swallow the lump in my throat as the elevator pings and the doors open.

"You going up to the happy hour after you drop off your art supplies?" he asks.

I nod. I know Al wanted to give me a sendoff. It's strange how close I've become to everyone in a matter of weeks. I've never felt more connected to a group of people than I have with everyone in this building. It makes me feel a little better knowing I'm leaving Aunt Cornelia in such good hands.

I drop my things and am surprised when I see my aunt with her walker.

"Get Kasen," she demands.

I turn and Kasen stops opening his door and steps back into the hallway.

"Everything OK, Cornelia?" he asks as he pokes his head into the apartment.

"I'm going to this happy hour. But the elevator doesn't go to the roof, so you'll need to carry me," she says with a wink.

Oh God. Did she have to wink?

Kasen chuckles. "I can do that. Come on," he says as he waves his hand. She hobbles over and he helps her to the elevator.

"I'll meet you all upstairs," Margie yells from the bathroom.

"OK," I reply.

I drop my things by the door and check myself in the

hallway mirror. I sweep my hair back up in a bun because it looks a mess.

"You coming up, illustrator?" Kasen's voice calls out. I'm going to miss his nicknames for me too.

"Yeah," I answer as I hurry to join them. The elevator starts buzzing and I hop inside. It lurches upward and my aunt lets out a long breath.

"This thing scares the shit out of me," she admits. "Someday, someone is going to get trapped in here."

Kasen laughs. "Hutch got trapped in here with Cam and Drew last year. And I think Bray the year before. Remember?"

"Oh, yeah, but only for thirty minutes," she points out.

"Well, the way Hutch explains it, they might as well have been trapped inside for two days," Kasen says.

I'm not going to lie, I have an immense sense of relief when the door opens. I practically run out and throw myself on the floor.

"OK, Piper, grab her walker. And I will carry Cornelia," Kasen states as he effortlessly picks up my little, old aunt. She grins up at him and I roll my eyes.

Kasen winks at me and I give him a shake of my head as I pick up the walker. When we get to the roof, everyone sees Cornelia and applauds.

"Why are we clapping for Miss Cornelia?" Ava asks. She's sitting on Bray's lap, coloring something.

"Because Miss Cornelia finally gets to come back up to a happy hour," Carly explains.

"I'm going to set you down here," Kasen says as he puts her on the nearest seat at the table with an umbrella.

I set the walker down next to her.

"Cornelia, your usual?" Al calls out.

"Nope, we're breaking out the champagne," Margie says as

she walks out of the stairs and holds up two big bottles of champagne.

"Damn, Margie! You've been lifting some serious weights if you were able to bring those things up here," Hutch says as he walks over to help her.

Hutch sets one bottle down and pops the cork on the other one. Ava cheers.

"Wait! I don't get any?" Ava asks once Al pours us all a glass.

I watch Al lean down, grab some ginger ale, and pour a little maraschino cherry juice in it.

"I made you a special drink," he says as he pops one cherry on top and hands it to Ava.

She claps excitedly. "Thanks, Mr. Al!" She pulls him down for a kiss on the cheek. He blushes.

"You're very welcome, Ava," he replies as he walks back over to grab his glass. "To having Cornelia back on the roof!"

"To Cornelia!" everyone says in unison.

"And to wishing Piper bon voyage as she heads to Seattle this week," he adds.

There is a wave of "good luck" and "we'll miss you" as everyone raises their glasses again.

"Thank you," I say shyly, a blush creeping up my cheeks from all the attention.

There's a pause which is quickly replaced by five or six different conversations. Troy, Jessa, Margie, and Aunt Cornelia start talking about a show they are watching. Drew and Cam are debating something about a book with Gray and Roxy. Bray is helping Ava color while talking to Hutch and Carly. Al is asking Kasen something, and I'm standing here next to Kasen, taking it all in.

I honestly don't know what I'm going to do without all of them.

"You look sad, Miss Piper. You want my pink drink?" Ava asks.

"Oh, thanks, Ava. I'm just sad to be leaving, but you keep your drink," I assure her.

"Wait! I can go get bubbles," she squeals and then leans toward me. "All the grown-ups here love bubbles. Miss Cam and Mr. Drew had a whole fight about who blew better bubbles. But I brought up my big bubble blower and I won."

Carly starts choking on her drink and Bray pats her back.

I look at them, not understanding.

"Sure, kiddo. Let's go get your bubbles," Bray says as he scoops her up and carries her downstairs.

I lean in toward Carly. "I'm sorry, what?"

She bursts out laughing. "Oh God! I'm so sorry! Cam, Drew, you guys suck!"

Cam starts laughing and Drew just shrugs and turns to me. "We needed a code phrase for a blowjob and blowing bubbles made sense, except someone's kid here had to be all like, 'I'm the best at blowing bubbles.' Anyhow, she was, but now it's sort of an inside joke," he explains.

"Oh, that's uh...OK," I say as I bite my bottom lip. I glance up and Kasen is watching me. I blush again and he leans down to my ear. "I think you are definitely the best at blowing bubbles."

Now my face is on fire.

"What did Kasen just say to you?" Drew asks, his eyebrows rising with suspicion.

I'm saved by a screaming Ava who runs back up with her giant bubble wand. "I got it! Drew, you want to compete?" she yells.

Carly looks wide-eyed at Bray. "Did you just IV her with sugar?"

"Mom!" Ava yells. "Unca Bray gave me this!" She pulls out one of those straws filled with flavored sugar.

"Mystery solved," Hutch laughs.

"Bray!" Carly scolds.

"She asked me for one the other day and I promised I'd buy it. She did do really good at school last week," he says with a shrug.

Carly slaps her forehead. "I swear, you're like the bad grandparent. Ava, sweetie, can you let me try it?"

"Sure, Mom. Here." She hands her mom the giant straw. "Come on, Mr. Drew. I'm totally winning blowing bubbles today."

"Yeah, Drew, show her your bubble-blowing skills," Hutch teases.

Drew glares at him.

"Why do you guys always look so mad about blowing bubbles?" Ava asks as she yanks on Drew's hand.

"Mr. Drew is just really competitive about his bubble blowing," Cam says with a smirk. Drew flicks her off once Ava turns around.

Cam gives him a big cheesy grin and Drew mouths, "You are so fucking dead later."

She blows him a kiss and we all giggle.

Kasen pats the stool vacated by Ava and Bray. "Have a seat."

"Pizza night!" Al declares, and with a few requests yelled, he orders us dinner.

---

Pizza night rolls into s'mores night and then one by one everyone heads downstairs until it's just Al, Kasen, Margie, Roxy, Gray, and Aunt Cornelia.

"I have a few authors who asked about your work. Should I send them to your website to contact you?" Roxy asks.

I raise my eyebrows. We've been up here for hours and she just brought this up now!

"Of course! That's great news. Thanks, Roxy," I say.

She leans over and whispers in my ear. "Sorry, I should have started with that, but Gray and I were pre-gaming tonight and I think I've had three too many."

"What's that? You want to practice bubble-blowing with me?" Gray says with a smirk.

Roxy laughs. "Nice try," she says. "We should head down though. It's getting late."

"Yeah, it's time to shut this party down," Margie declares.

Al looks from Kasen to me. "You kids can stay up. I'll get Hutch to bring Cornelia down."

"It's OK," Kasen says.

"You rang?" Hutch's voice calls out from the door to the stairs.

"It's your lucky night," my aunt says.

"My lady," Hutch plays along as he lifts her up with ease in one hand and then lifts the walker in the other.

"Why is he so big?" I mutter taking in Hutch's full strength.

Kasen leans in. "Hey, you're crushing my ego."

I turn to him. "Shall I kiss it and make it all better?"

He groans and I look over to see Al smiling at us. "Goodnight, Al."

"Till next time," he says and leans down to kiss me.

I snuggle up to Kasen's side. "So tell me all about this island near Seattle," he demands, and as if we've known each other for a lifetime, I lean against his shoulder and tell him about my dad's place. At some point, I fall asleep. I'm only vaguely aware of someone carrying me and tucking me into bed. A big warm body wraps around mine and I fall into the deepest sleep where I dream of a handsome, muscular man with dark eyes and dark hair.

# CHAPTER TWENTY-SEVEN

Kasen

I couldn't bring myself to bring her back to Cornelia's. Instead, I brought her to my bed where I had the best sleep I've had in days. Smelling her floral shampoo when I woke was like icing on the cake.

"Wake up, Sleeping Beauty," I whisper in her ear.

"Ten more minutes, Dad," she grumbles and I tickle her side.

"Stop!" she says, laughing. She rolls to face me, her green and blue eyes staring up at me.

Her laughter dies as I stare down at her. "You're beautiful, Piper. You know that?" I say.

She shoves my chest. "I'm just average. I mean other than my heterochromia."

"Huh?" I ask.

"My weird eye thing," she reiterates. So that's what it's called.

"No, you're beautiful. And not just on the outside." My

finger lazily traces her breast but my eyes stay fixed on hers. "Don't ever forget that, OK."

"I won't," she whispers.

"Good. Now, I think you need some morning sex practice," I say as I pull back the blanket. The heaviness between us dissipates as I kiss my way down her neck, lavishing each of her breasts before landing between her legs. I love the little moans she makes and the way her hands grip my hair as I taste her. I'm going to miss every little thing about this.

"Kasen!" she cries out as I taste her release on my tongue.

"Too much," she mumbles, trying to pull me away from her. But I keep going until she cries out again. Then I get up and haul her out of bed and into my shower, where she returns the favor and I introduce her to shower sex.

Once we're clean, I walk her to Cornelia and Margie's door. "I'll see you tonight," I say as I lean in and give her a quick kiss.

"Did I get an A in morning sex?" she teases.

"You got an A-plus and an A-plus for shower sex," I reply.

She grins and I pat her butt and send her inside the apartment. I know for a fact that I'll be thinking about her all day long.

———

It takes me a few hours, but I decide on a trendy restaurant and then the art museum that Piper mentioned as our third date. I rifle through my closet, feeling like a teenager going out with the girl I've pined over for months. I'm being ridiculous. In another day, she'll be gone.

I curse as I remember it's time for my therapy. I promised Bray that I would give it three months. We are almost through with month one and I'm not hating it. It's hard to accept my defects and accomplishments. I have realized that

I hate failing because then I'm not good enough. Not being able to save my parents and my friend made me want to always be perfect, so I don't ever want to fail that way again. I always knew I was being ridiculous but talking through it has helped. And because I'm so hard on myself, accepting praise is challenging. I'm always operating in a mode of "I can do better."

I toss my date clothes on the bed and log in for my appointment.

My therapist, Randy, is waiting.

"Hey, how are you doing this week?" he asks.

I shrug. "A little bummed but ready for my life to go back to normal, I guess," I admit.

"Back to normal?" he asks.

"Yeah, remember I mentioned that I was helping out that woman I just met?" I state while running my finger over a photo of Piper on my phone.

"Right. But I thought that was just showing her the dating ropes," he says. His dark eyes look at me through the screen and I hate that he's already seeing all my fissures on our fourth appointment.

"It was...I mean, it is," I correct, closing the photo app on my phone.

"That doesn't sound done," Randy says as he pushes his glasses up his nose.

I look out my window and watch a flock of birds fly into the park. It must be nice just to be able to pack up and fly away from your troubles.

"Kasen?"

My focus shifts back to Randy. "It has to be done."

"Why?" he asks.

"Because you've heard my issues. And my work is crazy. This woman...she's everything good and pure about the world. She deserves better. She deserves everything," I ramble.

"Then, doesn't she deserve you? If that's what she wants," he points out.

"She deserves better than me," I argue, practically growling because Piper deserves the sun, moon, and stars.

Randy raises a dark eyebrow. "So who should she date?"

"No one," I growl and immediately regret showing all my cards, even if I am paying this guy to help me sort out my feelings.

"I see," he says in a knowing voice.

I pinch the bridge of my nose. "I'd rather not talk about it. She leaves on Thursday morning," I state.

"Fine. We can move on, but remember, you don't get to pick who she wants to be with. And if she wants to be with you and you turn her down, then she can be with anyone else," he says and I hate that he's speaking the truth. I also hate how I feel. I don't want her to leave. I want her here in my bed, tucked safely against me every night. I want to sit on the bench in the park and watch her paint. But instead of saying that out loud, I circle back to my military trauma and we spend the rest of the call talking about one of the worst days of my life because right now, that seems less daunting than discussing my intensifying feelings for Piper.

———

"After you," I say as I press the small of Piper's back, guiding her inside the elevator. She's wearing heels today and I don't want her tripping on the stairs.

She steps inside and I follow her, pressing the down button. The elevator lurches down and then comes to a complete stop.

"Shit," I mutter.

"Uh, is that normal?" Piper asks, her voice rising an octave.

I jam my finger against the down button but nothing happens. Sighing, I pull out my cell phone and call Troy.

"Hey," Troy answers. "What's up? Tank spring a leak again?"

"Nope. Elevator's stuck," I say, my jaw clenching because nothing makes me more uneasy than a situation I can't control.

"Shit. OK, just you in there?" Troy asks and I can hear him moving around.

"Nope. Piper is here too," I state as I look down at her. She looks panicked. I place my hand on her back and gently rub it while I turn my attention back to Troy's voice. "I think we're between the third and fourth floors."

"Got it. I'll call the emergency line for the elevator people. If we can't get it moving, I'll need to call the fire station to come over here," he says as if he's done this one hundred times, and maybe he has.

"OK, keep me posted, please," I say as I hang up and look down at Piper.

Her chest is rising and falling quickly and I'm worried she's going to have a full-blown panic attack.

"Hey," I say and she looks up at me with those blue and green eyes. "Troy will have us out of here in a few minutes.

"Breathe, Piper," I state as I see her chest failing to rise. She sucks in a deep breath and looks around us.

"Now what?" she asks. I grin and open the door to the little telephone in the elevator. Two years ago, Bray had to use it when Troy was visiting his brother.

I pull out a deck of cards that Bray put in the telephone compartment after he got stuck. He had decided we needed something to do the next time it stopped working. "We could play strip poker."

She gives me a pointed look and I chuckle. "Fine, we can play..." I trail off as I try to think of something other than strip poker because the thought of Piper naked right now is the only thing my brain can process.

"How about go fish?" she suggests.

Now, I'm the one raising an eyebrow. She gives me a cute pout and I groan as I sit down and start shuffling cards.

She looks down at my lap and then up at me and I hold up my finger and motion to her to come sit in my lap. She gives me a small smile and sits down between my legs, leaning her head back on my chest.

"Don't cheat, OK," she says as she steals a glimpse of her cards.

I chuckle and press a kiss to the crown of her head. "I'll do my best."

She elbows me in the ribs.

I grunt. "Careful, illustrator," I growl.

She giggles. "Do you have a two?" she asks.

I hold my cards above her head and she tries to look at them. I tickle her side and she shoves at my hand.

Finally, I give up and wrap my arm around her arms and breasts, caging her in place. She squirms.

"No fair," she mutters.

Laughing some more, I say, "No, go fish."

She attempts to reach the discard pile of cards but a knock on the elevator has her pausing.

"You guys OK in there?" Troy asks.

"We're good. Just playing cards," I say loudly as I hear him trying to pry open the elevator doors.

"Damn, I think we're going to need that crank thing the fire station has. I'll call over there and then put a work order in with the elevator tech," he says. "Hold tight, I'll be back in a bit."

"Thanks," I say, keeping my arm wrapped around Piper.

She wiggles her ass against my groin and I feel the blood flowing toward my dick.

"Piper," I growl in her ear. She wiggles again.

"What?" she asks, feigning innocence.

"You know what," I murmur, while setting down my cards. Two can play at this game and I have the upper hand.

I take my free hand and slide it up her thigh, pushing her panties aside and running my fingers through her damp folds. She lets out a small whimper.

"You're wet for me," I whisper.

"Yes," she answers as I push one finger inside her. "Kasen," she manages.

"Shhh. We have time," I assure her.

"But..." She trails off as I slide a second finger inside her. Part of me wants to splay her out on the floor and taste her, but I sort of like having her locked against me. I like feeling her willingly give up control to me as I pleasure her.

"That's right, baby. Feel how good that is," I say as I use my thumb to circle her clit.

Her breath hitches and she grips my thighs. I can feel her chest rising and falling against my arm that's wrapped around it.

"You're so close. Grind against my hand," I demand. She pushes her pelvis against me and I feel her muscles begin to clench.

Her head tips back and her mouth falls open in a silent cry, her body trembling against me. Then she slumps back, breathing hard. I pull my fingers from her and suck them clean.

"That'll have to do for now," I declare as I loosen my grip on her. In the distance, I hear the sirens.

I straighten her panties and dress. I'm about to help her to stand when there's a noise from the elevator roof. We both look up and then at each other.

"Troy?" I ask.

It's silent and then we hear, "meow."

"Licorice?" I ask.

"Gray and Roxy's cat?" she questions as I help her to stand, while I start examining the small opening in the ceiling of the elevator that's currently closed.

"Yep," I explain as I reach up and then grab my pocket knife on my keyring to unscrew the panel. I begin to lift it down when suddenly a whole bunch of stuff falls down into the elevator.

"Look out," I say as I step back and put an arm out to protect Piper. Random artifacts rain down from the top of the panel I just removed. I set it down and we look at the items on the floor. There are cat toys, candy wrappers, screws, a half-eaten Twizzler, two gumballs, a bracelet made of beads, a pen, some tips from one of those cake piping things, four hair ties, a piece of newspaper, a cork from a wine bottle, and a few other items that are half-covered by things.

"No fucking way," Piper whispers loudly as she leans over and picks up a necklace, and not just any necklace, Cornelia's missing necklace.

"Meow!"

We both look up and see two green eyes staring down at us.

"Licorice!" I scold.

The cat begins to jump down and I quickly catch it. It grips on to me, and I yelp as it embeds its nails into my shoulder.

"Fuck!" I yelp.

Licorice uses me a springboard and jumps back up through the hole in the elevator ceiling.

"It's OK, sweetie," Piper coos. I glare at her as I try to inspect my shoulder.

"What about me?" I grumble.

"Oh, come here, I'm sure you're going to be fine," she says as she pulls on my shirt. "Can you just take your shirt off so I can examine it?" she asks, stuffing the necklace into a pocket on her dress.

I unbutton my shirt and peel it off.

"Oh, shit, he really got you," she says.

"She," I correct, grimacing as she touches the back of my shoulder.

"Hold on," she says as she carefully pulls off her dress. My mouth falls open as I take in her sexy matching underwear. It's white and lacey and barely hides her flesh.

She takes the skirt and spreads it apart, revealing two layers of material. She presses the inside layer against my shoulder and I hiss.

"Don't be a baby," she says.

"It stings," I mutter through clenched teeth.

"Oh, shit, the necklace," she curses and drops to her knees to pick it up just as the elevator doors open and four firemen and Troy look inside.

"Fuck," I mutter.

Piper squeaks and presses her dress against her nearly naked body.

"Sorry," a fireman says as they all look anywhere but at us.

Piper pulls her dress back over her head and stands. Her face is more red than a bottle of ketchup.

"I got a cut," I explain. "She was using her dress to stop the bleeding."

They all look back and I turn and point to my shoulder.

Troy looks up. "Is that Licorice? Did she scratch you or did the panel fall on you?"

"Meow!"

Sighing, I point to the cat and then the floor. "She's apparently been keeping all her toys up there," I explain as I pick up my shirt and put it back on.

"We found my aunt's necklace," Piper adds as she points to the necklace she's now wearing.

"Oh, that's great. Uh, if you can help lift her, we can get her out of here," a fireman says as he motions to Piper. I don't like the idea of him touching her, but we do need to leave. So I hoist her up and they pull her out. A minute later, they help me and tend to my cat scratches.

After Piper and I give them an awkward "thank you," we head out on what is left of our date. When we reach the sidewalk, Piper looks up at me. "I think after that, I'm officially prepared for any type of future date. Also, I can never look Troy in the eyes again."

I start laughing, and eventually, she joins me. "Come on, illustrator, I think we can still make the museum portion of this date. We can grab food at Joe's Tavern after." And as we walk to the museum, hand in hand, I'm overcome with sadness that this perfect woman will be leaving in less than twenty-four hours.

# CHAPTER TWENTY-EIGHT

Piper

It's Kasen's finger running lazily up and down my back that wakes me. For as un-practiced as I was with sex before these last five weeks, I now feel comfortable and confident about it. Last night, we spent nearly zero time sleeping and most of the time touching, kissing, and checking everything off a list I shared with him. While we ate at Joe's Tavern, he asked me what else I wanted to practice. I was embarrassed to share my list with him. Heck, I'm sort of embarrassed I have a list. But ever since I discovered romance books as a teenager, I've sort of kept a list of things I wanted to try someday. There were only a few of them left on the list, but Kasen spent all night making sure I experienced each and every one of them. He had told me that I needed to come up with a new list after we checked off the last one. But coming up with a new list means it won't be with him and that made me sad.

His finger stops as I blink. The sun is up but I can tell it's still early by the angle of the sun streaming through the blinds.

"Don't stop," I murmur as I snuggle against him, trying to memorize the feel of his body.

But he does. I start to look up at him, but he rolls me over, so I'm underneath him. He wedges himself between my legs and slowly sinks inside me.

I release a long breath as I spread my legs to make room for him. His gaze stays locked on mine as he begins to move at a languid pace. I wrap my legs around his waist and he leans down and kisses me.

Everything about this seems so real. This moment doesn't seem like practice at all. It feels as if we're really together and he's making love to me. I try not to come because I don't want this to end. I don't want him to stop looking at me like I'm the sun in his world.

"Hey," he says softly and wipes a stray tear away from the side of my face.

"I'm going to miss you," I admit.

He closes his eyes as if in pain. "I'll miss you too, illustrator," he finally says as he slowly opens his eyes. He pushes deeper inside me, and I thrust up to meet him. He uses one hand to reach between us, gently circling my clit until I can't hold back any longer. My eyes squeeze shut involuntarily as my release takes over just as Kasen grunts an expletive and pushes inside me deeply one last time. He stays there and I can feel him pulse as my muscles undulate around him.

He presses his forehead to mine and we stay like that for a while. Neither of us speaks, yet it feels like we're saying good-bye. Is this how relationships end? Is this practice for the next time I break up with a guy or he stops calling me?

But then Kasen pulls out of me and gets out of bed. "Come on, let's shower," he suggests.

I follow him into the bathroom where we take our time

washing and shampooing each other. He dries me off as if I'm made of glass and will break if he presses too hard.

Then I throw my clothes back on and walk to his door. Turning, I look up at him. He reaches out and caresses my cheek with the back of his hand.

"Safe travels, Piper," he says. He leans forward and kisses my lips. But instead of deepening the kiss, we both just stand there with our lips touching, neither of us moving for long seconds.

When he pulls back, he gives me a smile that doesn't reach his eyes. "Goodbye."

I swallow a lump in my throat. If he's saying goodbye, then he means it. Our practice relationship is over.

"Goodbye, Kasen," I say in a barely audible voice as I quickly turn and leave, forcing myself not to look back as I open my aunt's door and grab a change of clothes from my bag before locking myself in the bathroom to change and to let my tears flow freely.

"How was your night?" Aunt Cornelia says from her chair where, from the sound of her voice, she's clearly just woken up.

"Fine, thanks. I'm just going to get ready for my flight," I manage.

I furiously wipe at my tears, angry at myself for falling for a man who only promised to teach me to date. He never promised me his love in return.

I should be happy to have had him, to have had a friend like him. But instead, my heart is broken into a thousand little pieces. I should have just told him. I should march my ass back over there and tell him that I've fallen for him.

Placing my hand on the doorknob, I contemplate it. But then I chicken out. I focus on changing and brushing my hair, pulling it into a messy bun on top of my head.

I exit the bathroom after brushing my teeth and quickly

pack my suitcase. Then, taking a deep breath, I walk into the living room and try to give Aunt Cornelia a big smile.

"You need anything before I leave?" I ask.

She looks at me suspiciously and then at my neck.

"Oh, oops. I almost forgot. Guess what I found last night. We got stuck in the elevator and uh...anyhow, I found your necklace," I stammer as I take it off and hand it to her.

She doesn't accept it. Instead, she wraps my hand around it. "You keep it, Piper. Your uncle Bob would have loved seeing you wear it."

I frown as I open my hand and look down at it. It's so tied to her. "I—I can't. It's yours," I splutter.

"Come here," Aunt Cornelia says in her crackly, old voice.

I take the seat next to her. "Are you sure you want to leave?"

I press my lips together because deep down, my mind is screaming "No!" but instead I just nod.

"I see. Well, if you change your mind, you're always welcome here, Piper," she says as she pats my hand.

"Thank you," I reply and I secure the necklace back around my neck.

"You off to the airport?" Margie asks as she walks in from the kitchen.

"Yeah. I should probably head over there. Thanks for letting me keep my car here and tell Al thanks for letting me use the extra parking spot," I answer. Standing, I lean down and hug my aunt.

"I'll miss you, beautiful girl. Just remember, trust your instincts. You see more than you think," she whispers in my ear, and I have to fight back tears.

"OK," I reply. I walk over, hug Margie, and order a car.

Instead of taking the elevator, I start down the stairs with my suitcase. Hutch is coming up the stairs and sees me.

"Can I carry that for you?" he asks and then looks past me as if he's expecting to see someone.

"That'd be great. Thanks," I say as I hand him the bag. We start walking down the stairs and Hutch acts like my fifty-pound bag weighs nothing.

"So, you're heading to Seattle?" Hutch asks as we walk outside.

"Yeah, hopefully I'll be able to see my dad a bit," I say but my voice makes me sound unsure of myself.

"Oh," Hutch says with a sad smile. "I'd sort of hoped you'd stick around here."

I return his sad smile with one of my own. "I...no, I should go. Thanks, Hutch." I lean up and give him a big hug and he lifts me off the ground.

"Be safe, Pipes. I'll let you know if I find the flower person," he says as he motions toward the park with his head. He sets me down and I laugh.

"OK, you do that. I'll see you around," I say, not able to tell him a proper goodbye.

"Hey! Are you leaving?" Roxy's voice calls out from her store's door.

"Yes. My car should be here in a minute," I say as I check my phone.

"I'll text you later. A few more authors said they were interested in working with you," she says with a bright smile, her ponytail swinging behind her head.

"Thanks, Roxy. That's awesome news. I guess I'll see you guys next time I visit," I say because that makes this parting feel less permanent which makes me feel less sad.

"Of course," she says as she walks over and hugs me.

"Why are you all hugging Miss Piper?" Ava's voice calls out from a window above us.

"Shouldn't you be getting ready for school?" Hutch yells.

"It's a teacher something day. So no school," she replies. I look up to see her leaning out her window alongside a stuffed donkey.

"Ava, so help me, if you fall out of that window with Mr. Pickles, I am going to beat your ass," Hutch yells.

Ava giggles. "You said ass!"

"Ava, what in the..." We all hear Carly.

She joins her daughter in leaning out the window. "Where are you going?" Carly asks.

"To stay with my dad," I answer just as my car pulls up. Hutch starts loading my suitcase.

"We'll miss you," Carly says.

"Will you come back and blow bubbles with me?" Ava asks.

Hutch starts laughing silently and Roxy and Carly fight grins.

"Of course," I say, my cheeks turning bright pink.

I wave to all of them and get in the car. I can't look back as we drive away just like I couldn't look back when I said goodbye to Kasen. My gut tells me I'm making the biggest mistake of my life by leaving, but I also feel like a ship bobbing in the night if I stay. I have no real direction. What would I even do? And so, I slide my phone into my backpack and watch the city disappear as we drive out of town to the airport, memories of my last five weeks play like a film in my mind and tears slide down my cheeks.

# CHAPTER TWENTY-NINE

Kasen

There's a knock at my door. I'm in no mood to talk to anyone, but I so desperately am hoping that Piper changed her mind and stayed that I open it without looking.

I sigh when I realize it's just Hutch.

"Damn, glad to see you too," he says as he pushes in past me.

"Please, come in," I grumble as I shut the door.

"Can you tell me why Piper just got in a car and left for the airport?" Hutch asks, his arms crossed and his face serious.

"Because she's going to her dad's," I answer. But inside, I'm thinking, *because I'm an idiot and let her go. And I'll never forgive myself for not giving us a real chance, even though I still think she's better off without me.*

He holds up his hand. "Nope. Stop that right there, fuck-wad. You are a total idiot if you are letting her go."

"Geez, thanks," I mutter.

"I'm serious, bro. She's your perfect match. She made you light up. I've never once seen you as happy as you are when she's around," he says.

"Hutch, it was pretend. I was helping her out. I was giving her dating lessons and stuff," I say, glossing over the sex that happened between us.

He raises an eyebrow. "Right. How long do you plan on lying to yourself?"

"I'm not lying."

"You know, for someone who is a million times smarter than me, you are a real stupid fucker. You may have started out playing some 'big brother, I'll show you the ropes' man, but somewhere along the line, you fell for her and she fell for you. This stopped being pretend days ago, maybe a week or two ago or more. Do you seriously want to give all that up? Not even give it a go? For what? Because you think she deserves something else?" he says.

"She deserves better. What if I can't give her everything she needs?" I explain, admitting my feelings to my friend for the first time.

"Remember when you first got Napoleon?" Hutch asks as he walks over to my tank.

"I almost killed the poor guy," I state dryly.

"Exactly. Almost. But you figured it out. You worked hard to save him and look at him now. Happy as a...sea anemone," Hutch says, slowing down over the last few words.

"Mate, it was a pet. Piper is a person," I say, not getting his analogy at all.

"I'm trying to say that when something is important to you, you do everything you can to make sure it's alright. Relationships are hard, but I've already seen how you've changed. You protect her; you look out for her; you rearranged your schedule to be there for her. How is that not being the person she deserves?" Hutch asks.

I sit down on my sofa. "You're right," I finally state. Because he is right. I did a lot of things just to help her because I care about her. *Fuck. I love Piper. I need her. She needs me. What the hell have I done?*

I stand abruptly. "I need to get her back!"

"Now that's what I'm talking about. Let's go. Uh, we need Bray's car," Hutch says. He pulls out his phone and texts. "OK, he's meeting us downstairs. Let's go."

"We?" I ask.

"Yeah, *we*. You need to buy yourself a ticket to Seattle, right now," Hutch instructs. I get on my phone as we walk downstairs and find that there are a handful of tickets left on what I assume is her flight. I buy one.

Bray's already parked out front in his fancy sports car which is completely impractical for city driving.

"Get in, losers, we're going to get Kasen's woman," Bray calls out from the driver's seat.

I look at Hutch, a man that makes even me seem normal-sized.

"I'll fit," he says, as if reading my mind.

"How? Is this a clown car?" I quip.

"Just get the fuck in," he mutters as he climbs into the back. He has to keep his head ducked down and he looks ridiculous. "Bray?"

Bray turns around. "Do not get in an accident."

Bray laughs. "Right. Come on, Kase."

I climb in and he takes off at Mach speed down the street and straight to the airport.

The entire ride is Bray and Hutch coaching me on what to say, which ranges from ridiculous love sonnets to baring my heart.

"None of that works," I say as Bray pulls off onto the airport exit.

"Fine, then just tell her the truth. Speak from the heart,

man," Hutch insists. Flashes of recent conversations with Randy, Al, Cornelia, and Cam come rushing back to me. They were all correct. Maybe I needed Piper as much as she needed me. Maybe we both still need each other.

*God, I hope she still wants me. Did she want me before? Fuck it. It's now or never.*

Bray pulls up to the airport in record time, peeling into a free spot along the curb.

"Go get your woman," he says.

I get out of the car. "I have no idea what I'm doing," I admit in a moment of weakness.

Hutch looks up at me. "You're going and getting the woman of your dreams. Now, go, go get her."

I close my eyes and inhale. The air is filled with exhaust but somehow my mind smells floral shampoo, and I know that I need to smell that damn shampoo every day for the rest of my life.

"OK," I say, mostly to myself, but Hutch fist-pumps.

"Hell, yeah!" he yells.

I run into the airport and get to security. There's a long line and I groan as I check the time. The plane is already starting to board. I rush to the front of the line.

"Excuse me, I'm running really late. Flat tire. Any chance I can just get through really quick?" I ask a woman who gives me a look.

"Sir, the line starts back there," she says pointing to where I was.

I swallow. *Fuck it.* "Listen, I know. And I hate to cut the line, but the woman I love is about to get on a plane and fly away and I can't let her go without telling her I love her. I bought a plane ticket just so I can go find her and hopefully talk her out of leaving," I say, feeling a little silly for baring my soul but also not giving a fuck.

The woman tilts her head to the side.

"Please," I beg.

"Let the man through," an old lady in line says.

"You can't ruin his shot at true love," a teenager calls out.

A few other passengers chime in with support.

"Fine, go," she grumbles, and I run up, toss my things in a bin, and go through the scanner.

And, it beeps. Whomp. Whomp.

"Sir, I'm going to need you to check your pockets," a surly-looking man says.

I do as I'm told, but don't find anything. Then I remember, my side pants pocket has my keys. Thank God I left my pocket knife at home!

I toss them in one of those little containers and walk back through the scanner. He waves me on, and I grab my keys and continue running to the gate. I make it just in time.

"Well, with only five minutes to spare," the flight attendant says.

I look up and realize the flight got bumped back five minutes. Thank the gods!

I walk onto the plane and search the rows. And then...I see her. She's sitting by a window, staring out, and...is she crying?

I wait as people put bags in the overhead compartments. Finally, I reach her row and slide past a college-aged kid sitting on the aisle. I sit down.

"You sad that there's no lily pads or frogs out there," I state.

Piper's head whips around toward me, her eyes wide and glimmering with tears. I reach out wiping a few away from her cheeks.

"Kasen?" she says, her hand coming out to touch my jaw as if she thinks I'm a mirage.

"Yeah, illustrator," I state as I search her eyes.

"What are you...why are you...how are you here?" she stammers.

I caress her cheek and smile. "I realized that you don't need to go to Seattle to figure out your life." I pause and restate what I'm thinking. "I don't want you to go to Seattle. I want you right here. I want to wake up and smell your shampoo. I want to watch you talk to my fish while you feed them. I want to sip whiskey with you. I want to sit in the park while you paint frogs. I want to drink coffee at Cam's café with you. I want...you." I trail off and search her eyes.

"You want me?" she asks as she frowns in confusion.

"Yes, I just want you, Piper. I never intended to find the one person who completes me. I know we were pretending but...somewhere along the way, I just...I fell in love with you. I didn't mean to. I didn't think I was good enough for you. But I want to be. You make me want to be better. I went to therapy because of you. I'm trying to fix myself because of you. I'm better because of you and if you give me a chance..." I trail off again overcome by emotion and my racing thoughts.

She places a finger over my lips. "You had me at *you fell in love with me*." She smiles. "I love you too, Kasen. I'm not exactly sure how that happened in a matter of weeks, but...it did." She has new tears falling but her smile tells me these are happy tears. "I'm a little scared," she admits.

"So am I," I admit.

"So...we're, like, going to give this a real try?" she asks.

"If you want to," I answer.

She grins and throws her arms around my neck. "Let's deboard. And go home."

"Home?" I ask.

"Yeah. Home," she says. We both get up and leave after a long discussion with the gate agent and having to get her bag out of the plane; thank God they were just loading it and

Piper faked a sob story about her aunt which was sort of true but also sort of a lie since she broke her ankle nearly six weeks ago.

"How are we getting home?" Piper asks as we walk out of the airport. I point to Bray's car.

"I called in a favor," I state as Hutch opens the passenger seat and takes Piper's suitcase while the two of us slide into the back seats.

"Welcome back, Piper," Bray says as he steers us home.

———

I breathe in the floral shampoo smell in her hair. It's been two weeks, and I feel like the whole world has changed. Piper moved in officially last weekend. I went and got her things from her mom's house. She keeps saying this is a trial thing, but I think that's just her defense mechanism. She doesn't want to end up like her parents and I totally get that.

Her business is booming. She has a dozen contracts with authors right now and she's also working on pieces for her first gallery showing next month. And in her spare time, she's decided to illustrate her own children's book about frogs that live in a pond in a park in a city.

I squeeze her a little, drawing her tighter against me.

"Good morning," she murmurs as she slides her leg between mine. Her hand goes up to my hair and she runs her fingers through the strands.

"Morning, baby," I say, adding a kiss to her head.

She sighs contentedly and kisses my chest, and I feel...at peace.

This is how happiness is supposed to feel. I'm still working on being happy and accepting myself, faults and all, but I'm getting there, slowly, very slowly.

"You're overthinking," Piper says with a laugh. "Get out of your head."

I smile and kiss her head again.

"I can be persuaded to get out of my head," I tease as I push my morning wood against her leg.

"You're insatiable, Kasen Saddler," she says and then sits up. "Oh God, I'm a terrible girlfriend."

"Why?"

"I don't even know your middle name," she says aghast as if that's a crime.

I chuckle. "Kasen Ian Saddler. What's yours?"

She blushes. "Octavia."

I raise my eyebrows.

"It's after an author my mom liked," she explains and then curls back up against me.

"You know what?" she asks.

"What?" I run my hand over her soft hair, wishing we could lie here all day.

"I'm glad Aunt Cornelia sent me to find her necklace. Because it made me find you," she says as she gives me a squeeze.

"I'm glad you found me too. And now that you found me, there's no letting go," I state.

"Never," she agrees. And we lie there for another hour, just holding each other. I'm not entirely sure why the universe saw fit to have me find this perfect woman, but I'm awfully glad it did.

## EPILOGUE

Piper

*Two months later...*

"Cam, make it a double shot," I say as Kasen and I stand in Cam's café waiting on our drinks and muffins.

"Sure thing," she says. She doesn't seem like her normal self today.

"What's wrong?" Kasen asks, clearly picking up on the off vibes as well.

She sighs as she hands us our drinks and muffins. Then she points to a building across the street and several doors down from our apartment building.

"I've heard a rumor that a corporate coffee place is going in there. How am I supposed to compete with that? I haven't even signed all the papers yet on this place and I may already have impossible competition," she says with a huff.

"Maybe it's just a rumor," I point out.

"Maybe everyone will love your place so much it won't even matter," Kasen offers.

"What's wrong?" Hutch asks as he walks in wearing full camo gear.

"Please tell us you are not still trying to find the Guardian of Hearts Lane Park?" Cam says to him.

He waves her off. "Yes, I am, but what's wrong?"

I point to the building across the way. "Cam thinks a corporate coffee place is moving in there."

"Oh...huh. That sucks. Maybe it won't," Hutch says.

"Where are you two off to?" Cam asks us.

"Going to check out the gallery for the exhibit," I say. Everyone knows my big art exhibit is this coming weekend.

"Can't wait to see the new stuff," Hutch says with a grin as Cam hands him his drink.

Al walks in and we all turn and wave at him.

"Good morning, everyone," Al says.

"Morning," we say in unison.

"Ready for the big show?" he asks me.

I nod. "Almost. You're coming, right?"

"I wouldn't miss it. How is the happy couple today?" he asks as he looks from Kasen to me.

Kasen pulls me against him. "Good. We're just heading over to the gallery now to check on a few things," he says.

"Did you hear the rumor about the corporate coffee place moving into our block?" Hutch asks Al.

"No, I hadn't heard anything," Al says with a surprised look.

I take a bite of muffin and moan. "Cam, there's no way a corporate place can compete with these muffins. What do you put in them, crack?" I ask.

"Yes, it's why they are so highly addictive," she says deadpan.

I giggle. "That explains everything."

"Come on, artist, let's go," Kasen says to me, and I smile up at him, loving my latest nickname.

"See you guys at happy hour?" I ask.

They all nod and we walk out to Kasen's car. It's only a two-minute drive to the gallery. He parks out front and we walk inside. I take a long moment to look at my work. I can't believe I'm getting my own exhibit.

Kasen comes up behind me and wraps his arms around my shoulders. "You did good, artist. It looks amazing," he says. "I'm so proud of you."

We walk around and I check the placement of a few pieces. And then we get to the one I wanted him to see first. It's a piece I've been working on when I can spare a few minutes from him.

He stops in his tracks and looks up at it. "It's... how...when?"

I grin. "When you were busy working." He walks over to it and examines it more closely. It's a portrait of us curled up in bed, the sun shining through a window. You can't really tell it's us unless you look closely.

I see the moment that he finds the little placard with the name of the piece. He turns to me and grins, and I grin back. Then he takes two steps toward me and takes me into his arms, kissing me deeply. He gives me one final peck and leans back, looking over again at the name of my painting.

"I'm buying this one," he says. "*Finding Romance* is coming with us on Saturday."

I hope you enjoyed this story. Ready for Cam's love story in Book 3, Building Romance? Order it now!

If you want more romantic comedies, you can start with my Perfectly Imperfect Love Series. In Book 1, a photographer has to move in with a baseball player. And don't forget to grab your free copy of the Meet-Cute Mishap by joining my newsletter, plus receive freebies, giveaways, and so much more!

USA Today & International bestselling romance author, S.E. Rose lives near Washington D.C. with her family. When she's not wrangling her cats or keeping up with her kids, she's plotting her next story.

She loves all things wine, coffee, and cats. In her non-existent free time, she enjoys traveling, going to concerts, binging on her favorite shows, and reading, especially if it's a good mystery or comedy.

Learn more about upcoming books from S.E. Rose at www.seroseauthor.com.

# ALSO BY S.E. ROSE

**Deceitful Destiny Series**
Island (Book 1)
Secrets (Book 2)
Bravura (Book 3)
Determination (Book 4)
Home (Book 5)

**The Poisoned Pawn World**
A Fierce Princess
A Valiant Prince
A Wise Prince
A True King
The Overnight Naughty List

**The Kingmakers of Kensington**
A Man of Power
A Man of Wealth
A Man of Prestige

**Perfectly Imperfect Love Series**

Undeniably Perfect
Hopelessly Perfect
Romantically Perfect
Awkwardly Perfect
Reluctantly Perfect

## Brides of Banneker

Scoring the One
Landing the One
Fixing the One

## Once Upon a Billionaire Rom-Com Series

The Billionaire and the Librarian
The Billionaire and the Maid
The Billionaire and the Runaway

## Romances in the Building Series

Faking Romance (Book 1)
Finding Romance (Book 2)

## Fanning the Flames Series (Co-authored with Sierra Hill)

Burned (Book 1)
Ignited (Book 2)
Scorched (Book 3)

## Clearview Falls University Series (Co-authored with Sierra Hill)

Falling for the Fake Boyfriend (Book 1)
Falling for the Roommate (Book 2)
Falling for the Football Player (Book 3)
Falling for the Quarterback (Book 4)

## Novels

Chronicles of a Hot Mess
Chronicles of a Rockin' Mess
The Decoy
Second Start (A Holiday Springs Resort Novel)
The Road Trip Romance

## Novellas & Short Stories
Neighbor in Apartment No. 5
The Tinsel Tango
The Fighter
A Polar Pursuit (Vagabond Series)
A Forward Holiday
Love in an Elevator
When It Rains, It Pours
Misery Loves Company

Want to learn more? Visit www.seroseauthor.com.

www.ingramcontent.com/pod-product-compliance
Lightning Source LLC
Chambersburg PA
CBHW030138010826
48973CB00002B/627